370

MILK FLOOD

MILK FLOOD

by Paul Corey

Illustrated by RAFAELLO BUSONI

 ABELARD-SCHUMAN, New York

CONTENTS

CHAPTER 1   *One-Can Crane*   9
2   *A Business Proposition*   16
3   *Milk Station*   21
4   *The Organizer*   27
5   *Strategy*   35
6   *Canning Factory*   42
7   *Shareholder*   49
8   *Trouble*   57
9   *Passing Inspection*   65
10   *The Opening*   75
11   *Yellow Gold*   82
12   *Written Agreement*   89
13   *"Joshua Fit The Battle"*   96
14   *The Long Ride*   104
15   *Debt Paid*   111
16   *More Trouble*   119
17   *Fire*   127
18   *One Mystery Solved*   134
19   *Co-operation*   141
20   *The Cows Come Home*   149
21   *Goals Reached*   156
22   *Emery Crane, Dairyman*   164
23   *The Fight*   172
24   *Grass Time*   183

MILK FLOOD

Chapter One

ONE-CAN CRANE

The white end doors of the big red barn were rolled back and the May wind blew down the alleyway between the two rows of empty stanchions. It brought the smell of spring flowers from the ridge meadow and mingled it with the smell of last year's hay and the cow smells of the dairy barn. A robin sang in the golden willow by the lane.

Emery Crane stopped sweeping the barn floor, stopped whistling exuberantly, and seemed to listen. His brown eyes gazed dreamily into the sunlight. He was eighteen years old, wiry and tall, his face as brown as an oak leaf in winter.

With the dairy herds in spring pasture the flow of milk was increasing. The milk flood had started. His three cows had produced a full can of milk—ten gallons, eighty-five pounds—with last night's and this morning's milkings. That was something to crow about.

Prince, a big shepherd dog, trotted up to the barn door, his job of driving the cows to pasture finished. A few minutes later Emery's chunky fourteen-year-old brother David appeared, hatless, his straw-colored hair wind-ruffled.

"Hey, Em, I saw a fox up by our sugarbush."

"Fox-smox, hurry up and take care of the calves."

"Okay, okay. 'One-can Crane' they call him now."

Grinning, Emery hung up the broom and hurried across the yard to the milkhouse. Everything was in order—the milking machines drained on their racks; pulsator heads, rubber tubes, and teat-cups, like great black spiders, dangled limply from hooks; the heavy cooler lid was closed tight.

He jotted down fourteen cans of milk for his father and one for himself on the milk chart. That was the "make" for the day as the dairymen said it. The sound of horse's hoofs attracted his attention and he looked out the window over the loading platform. A sorrel pony cantered into the yard, ridden by a slender girl wearing jeans and leather jacket, her black hair held by a red babushka.

"Hi, Mary!" Emery yelled.

Mary Spivac was Emery's age. Her eyes were startlingly blue in her dark face and her smile showed vividly white teeth.

"My three cows made a can of milk," Emery boasted. "First time they've made a whole can."

"Swell." Then the smile vanished from the girl's face. "The station sent our milk back yesterday morning."

"Sent it back! What for?"

"Mr. Bunce said it smelled. Ma and Dad and I couldn't smell anything bad."

"Gee, that's a shame, Mary."

The girl swung nimbly out of the saddle. "Mr. Muller stopped in yesterday afternoon. He smelled our milk and said it smelled all right to him."

"Muller has three big dairies; I'll bet Bunce doesn't send his milk back," Emery said.

"Mr. Muller said he'd see Mr. Bunce about our milk." Mary slapped the reins against her jeans; then she added: "We're going to sharecrop a patch of beans for him."

"Was that what Muller came to talk about?" Emery asked, and Mary nodded.

The big dairymen made a sideline of raising truck-garden produce for the New York market and got the small dairymen to sharecrop for them. The Cranes had never sharecropped vegetables.

"It's a gamble," Emery said.

"Mr. Muller says that green beans are going to bring a good price this year and Dad thinks a few acres might help us out if there's trouble in the milk shed."

Emery frowned. "Trouble in the milk shed" meant trouble in the wide area that supplied New York City with milk; it would mean trouble especially for small dairymen like his father. Something like that *would* have to happen just when he wanted to get started dairying on his own. "I hope they don't send your milk back *this* morning, Mary."

"You can say that again." Then, leading the pony, Mary headed across the yard to the house.

Emery watched her go. The Spivacs were a big family on a not-very-good farm. Last fall little Conrad Spivac had been trampled by their Ayrshire bull and they had a lot of doctor bills. It was pretty rough on them when the collection station of the Associated Dairymen rejected their milk.

Emery stopped thinking about the Spivacs when he began to bolt the sections of the disk harrow together, getting ready for spring field work: maybe now that his cows were making a full can of milk he ought to become a patron of the A.D. on his own and not sell his milk along with his father's. Then it occurred to him that his dad should be back from the station by this time and he glanced briefly toward the road.

Mary Spivac was riding out of the yard, carrying his mother's electric iron which she had come to borrow. He went over to service the big Farmall tractor and noticed his sister Bets and his brother David start down to catch the school bus. A frown of worry pinched his forehead: his dad *was* late this morning.

Just as he backed the tractor up to the disk harrow, the Crane's big green truck roared up to the milkhouse platform. A dull fear gripped Emery as he watched his father begin unloading the cans; they handled as if they were heavy. Maybe his dad had brought back several cans of hot water from the station. They did that sometimes. Automatically he counted—three, four. The fifth too was heavy. They had never brought home that much hot water.

Emery leaped off the tractor and ran across the yard. "What's in those cans, Dad?"

"Milk!" snapped his father. "Bunce sent it back."

"Did he send my milk back?"

"He sent it all back!"

Emery's mouth suddenly felt all dried up. "Why?"

Mr. Crane straightened up. He was a lean, strong man of forty; his tan face twitched with anger.

"Said it smelled!"

"Smelled!"

Emery searched out his can, pried up the cover and took a deep sniff. "I don't smell anything except good milk."

"Neither did I," growled Mr. Crane. "But Bunce said it smelled."

"We'll get Mom down here. She can smell." Emery cupped his hands to his mouth and yelled: "Mom! Mom!"

The back door of the stone house slammed and Mrs. Crane came out on the porch, wiping her hands on her apron.

"Mom, will you come smell the milk?"

She hurried toward them, a worried look on her round pink face that made her eyes unnaturally large behind her glasses. Emery and his father opened all the cans so she could smell the milk.

"Why'd they send it back?" she asked, but without waiting for an answer, she began sniffing. "It smells like good milk to me—all of it."

"Almost a hundred and fifty gallons—over a thousand

pounds; forty dollars worth." Mr. Crane's tone was bitter.

"They sent the Spivacs' milk back yesterday morning," Emery said. "That's what Mary told me."

Mr. Crane turned on him sharply. "They took it this morning. I saw them." Then he scowled. "Maybe the A.D.'s trying to soften up us little fellows for a price-cut."

"Why don't you protest, Lou?" asked Mrs. Crane.

"Protest! They wouldn't pay any attention to my protest. They're all big producers on the Committee and they run the A.D. hand-in-glove with the dealers and handlers."

"Well, they can't keep sending my milk back," Emery said. "I want money for my milk, I want to buy more cows."

"If this keeps up," replied his father, "we'll need every cent we can get from your cows as well as mine just to keep us afloat."

"I'd like to take a poke at Bunce," Emery said.

"He does what the Committee tells him to," Mr. Crane said. Then he added: "You put those cans in the cooler while I go up and call the Board of Health to come and check them."

Emery slammed up the heavy cooler lid and plunked the cans into the cold water one by one.

His father appeared at the door of the milkhouse and Emery looked up eagerly. "They coming out?"

"Yes." But Mr. Crane's lips curled. "Tomorrow. This milk will have spoiled by then; they wouldn't be able to tell whether it was bad this morning or not."

"What're we going to do with it?" Emery demanded.

"Separate the cream so your mother can churn it. We'll give the skimmed milk to the pigs."

"If that cheese factory in Atlas were running we could sell it there," Emery remarked hopelessly.

"Well, it isn't running. You'd better start disking that upper field for oats. I'll take care of this milk."

Emery walked out of the milkhouse. His first full can of milk was a total loss as far as he was concerned; as butter and pig feed it didn't mean anything to him. He shuffled dejectedly up the slope to the idling tractor.

Chapter Two

A BUSINESS PROPOSITION

All morning Emery kept the tractor and disk going back and forth around the contour of the hill field, chopping the old corn stubble. Once he stopped the rig at the ridge end above the farmyard where he got a sweeping view of the wrinkled, shaggy country that was central New York State.

Solid as the hills stood their story-and-a-half house built of yellow-gray limestone. This side of it lay the dark plot of garden which his mother and Bets had already planted. To the west was the orchard backed by a windbreak of locust trees whose half-dead limbs somehow retained a massive dignity as they towered against the sky. Beyond the house was the new barn and cement-block silo.

They were still in debt for those, Emery reminded himself, still plenty in debt.

His glance shifted to his father's wood lot and sugar-bush to the northeast and starting there he looked slowly around over the valleys fanning out to the south, spotting occupied farmyards: Meaney's, Shostikov's, Lane's. In this sweep of country he spotted a half dozen abandoned farms.

Across the road and below the drive to their yard was the unoccupied Armstrong farm. The four-room house was old and shabby, but the small barn, with stanchions for twelve cows, was still in fair condition.

Emery knew that barn well. He and David and Chuck Lane had spent many a rainy day in it. This old farm could be rented cheaply, even bought for a low price, and often this spring he had thought that if he had eight or ten cows he might rent it, fix up the barn, and start dairy-ing, while he continued to live at home, helping his father.

He compressed his lips. There wasn't any sense even thinking about that if trouble was brewing for the milk shed. He resumed disking.

At dinner that noon, Emery asked: "What'll we do if the A.D. rejects our milk tomorrow, Dad?"

"I asked the Board of Health to send out an inspector," replied Mr. Crane. "He can test it."

"Then we'll be able to find out what's wrong with it."

"There's nothing wrong with our milk," asserted his father. "The A.D. rejected it for a purpose. I don't know what that purpose is—yet. But they don't do that sort of thing up in St. Lawrence County where the farmers have Co-op dairies. The A.D. broke the small dairymen's organization down here once, but if they go on rejecting milk, we small producers will organize again."

Mrs. Crane looked worried. "That'll mean trouble."

"We're having trouble now, Mom," replied Emery.

Just as they finished eating, a shiny new car drove into the yard. "It's Mr. Muller," Mrs. Crane said.

Emery and his father went out to meet their visitor. He was a stocky man, about Mr. Crane's age, wearing neatly pressed khaki trousers and a leather jacket.

"I'm lining up some farmers to raise beans for me," he said. "That piece of yours down there on the flat"—he waved his stubby hand toward the five acres below the barn—"looks as if it would be good bean land."

"Sharecropping beans is too much of a gamble for us," Mr. Crane replied.

"This year's different," Muller said. "A lot of Jersey truck farmers have been flooded out and there'll be a good market."

Mr. Crane shook his head. "Too hard on the land."

"One year'll make little difference," argued Muller. "Next year may not be a good year and you can skip the beans."

"Look, Dad," Emery interrupted, "let me take that five acres and put it into beans. It'll be a—a hedge against any more milk trouble with the A.D."

"Bunce reject your milk?" Muller inquired casually.

"This morning—first time," admitted Mr. Crane.

"Bunce's got the jitters." Muller patted his crew-cut hair as if he were quieting a dog with raised hackles. "I've been expecting him to send some of my milk back. It always smells a little off when the cows first go out to grass. I'll have a talk with him about your milk." Then he added: "But the handlers are talking price-cut this spring and that five acres in beans might come in handy."

Emery remembered his talk with Mary: the Spivacs' milk was sent back; Muller called and wanted them to raise beans; he offered to talk to Bunce about their milk and they agreed to sharecrop some beans; this morning their milk had been accepted by the A.D.

"Dad, let's try it this year."

His father was frowning. "I'd figured on putting that piece in silo corn. I'll have to think it over."

"Sure." Muller grinned at Emery. "I'm just making you a business proposition. Think it over and let me know."

After he drove off, Emery said: "Let me make a project of it, Dad. Rent me the piece. Muller wants beans and maybe we could get him on our side against the A.D."

"He's a big milk producer," replied Mr. Crane, "and the Associated Dairymen is run for him and the big outfits like Biggart, Howells, and Leffinger."

"But Mr. Muller's not on the Committee," Emery argued. "That makes him sort of outside—on our side, maybe."

"Maybe. But sharecropping is just another way the big fellows have of getting a hold over us small operators. You'd better get on with your disking."

Emery walked up to the tractor. Muller predicted that this would be a good year for beans in the market. If his father would rent him that five acres he might be able to make enough profit to buy a couple more cows. He looked thoughtfully at the old Armstrong barn across the road; then he leaped up to the tractor seat and started the rig.

Chapter Three

MILK STATION

After breakfast the next morning, Mr. Crane said: "Guess you'd better come along with me to the milk station, Emery. I may need a witness to what's said."

Mrs. Crane searched his face in alarm. "Now, Lou, don't you lose your temper."

"Think they'll reject our milk again, Dad?" Emery asked anxiously.

"We'll find out when we get there."

The fifteen cans of milk—last night's and this morning's "make"—were already loaded on the truck. Mr. Crane drove the truck north past the Spivac place to the Four

21

Corners where they turned right on the main highway,
Route 20.

When the truck coasted down the long hill to the
railroad tracks at Atlas, Emery looked north to the abandoned Central New York Cheese Factory.

"Gee, I wish somebody would start that up again," he
remarked.

"If wishes were cows, beggars would need milking
machines," replied his father, frowning.

As they roared along toward Sheltonville and the milk
station, they passed one of J. Holland Muller's farms.
Near the highway were long sheds where the produce
from his sharecropped lands was collected for shipping
to the New York City market. Farther back stood two
huge barns and three silos. Beyond these, partially hidden
in a grove, were two rows of shacks which looked like
chicken houses. Muller housed his imported pickers and
truck-garden workers in these.

"Dad," Emery said, "if the A.D.'s going to keep on
rejecting our milk, we ought to take Muller's proposition."

"We'll wait and see what happens at the station."

In Sheltonville, Mr. Crane turned left past the Colonial
Inn and drove out toward the north edge of the village.
The white Associated Dairymen's milk station loomed
large ahead of them. Smoke poured from the tall black
stack in the rear. As they pulled in, a truck drove away
from the short roller conveyor line where the full cans
of milk were unloaded, and stopped at the end of the
long conveyor line across the yard where the sterilized,
empty cans were picked up again.

Emery helped his father unload the cans and watched

them slide along the conveyor to the swinging door in the station wall. When the last one disappeared, Mr. Crane drove the truck out into the yard. Then he remarked grimly: "We'd better go into the office and see what happens next."

As they approached the entrance, Nels Peterson came slamming out, his long neck and thin face red with rage.

"Twice this month he's rejected my milk, Lou," Peterson said fiercely. "And there's nothing wrong with it."

"He sent ours back yesterday, Nels," said Mr. Crane.

Peterson's bony fingers clutched Mr. Crane's shoulder. "I'm going to get hold of Percy Woods from St. Lawrence County. We'll organize again." He walked on.

Emery felt his body tighten all over as he continued with his father toward the office. As they reached the door, he heard a yell: "Hi there, Crane! How's your mastitis-riddled herd of cows?"

Whirling angrily around, Emery saw Delbert Bunce, chunky son of the manager of the A.D., talking with someone in the Spivac truck. Young Bunce was an old rival of his from high school days. Emery decided to ignore the dirty crack about the health of their herd of cows, but his face still burned as he watched the men in white overalls and boots swing the milk cans from the conveyor, dump them into the weighing machine, then send the empties clattering on to the sterilizer.

Where were their cans, Emery wondered. He looked for the black "77" marked on the shining metal containers. His glance shifted over the room, past the thousand-gallon storage tank to the refrigerating system which reduced the milk temperature before it was piped into the storage tank or into a tank truck which would haul it to New York City.

Then he saw short, fat Mr. Bunce coming toward them, walking with an easy roll. The affable grin on Bunce's face didn't seem quite genuine to Emery.

"Sorry about yesterday's milk, Lou," said Mr. Bunce. "It's okay this morning. Slightly tainted yesterday. Sometimes when you first let the cows out to pasture that happens." He didn't look up into their faces as he spoke. "We can't take chances. There's a surplus down in the City. And if we give 'em a chance they'll send a whole tank full back." Then he bustled through the door marked "Private."

Emery and his father walked out to their truck.

"I don't believe there was a thing wrong with our milk yesterday either," Emery said.

"I'm sure the A.D.'s trying to soften us up for a price-cut," replied his father. "Bunce tipped his hand when he talked about a surplus down in the City."

Cans "77" came steaming down the roller path from the sterilizer and Emery loaded them aboard the truck. A quick glance at the weight tag on one of the handles told him the poundage for the day: 1190 lbs. Eighty-five pounds of that milk was from his cows. But yesterday the same amount had been lost. How was a fellow to start dairying if he couldn't be sure of selling the milk he produced?

As they started to drive away, the big Muller Dairy truck swung into the yard, with Muller himself driving it. He pulled to a stop, got out and came to meet the Cranes.

"Morning, Lou. How're you, Emery? Bunce take your milk this morning?"

"He took it," said Mr. Crane.

"It was no different from yesterday's," Emery said.

"I don't doubt that." Muller chuckled. "Bunce is an old woman; the dealers have him scared to death." He frowned slightly. "Goin' to raise beans for me?"

Emery held his breath, waiting for his father to answer. "Em thinks he'd like to make a project of that five acres for you."

"Good. That's an easy way for a young fellow to get some quick money."

Young Bunce came away from the Spivac truck. "Morning, Mr. Muller," he said. "Did you bring the agreement for me to sign?"

"I'll bring it around," replied Muller. Then to the Cranes he said: "Del's putting in twenty acres for me." He turned back to young Bunce. "Emery's putting in five."

Bunce's lips curled. "Might make six hundred bucks with that. I'll make enough on my twenty to pay my first year at Cornell."

"Thought you'd given up going to college," remarked Muller.

"I just stayed out last year to help the old man around the station." Young Bunce ruffled his shock of red hair. "He doesn't need me now, so I'm going to be a college boy."

"And study what?" Muller was grinning.

"Agriculture. I'll come back here and tell these two-by-four dairy farmers how to do it."

"Guess there's a few you won't be able to tell anything, eh, Emery?" Muller winked at the Cranes.

Young Bunce swaggered off to the station office.

"He's getting too big for his breeches," remarked Muller dryly.

"Twenty acres of beans will keep him busy—may reduce him a little," said Mr. Crane, smiling.

"Not if I know him," replied Muller. "He'll be hiring the work done." Then he added: "I'll bring the agreement over for you to sign one of these days, Emery."

"Thanks, Mr. Muller." Emery felt better. Mr. Muller was friendly—he was on their side.

As they drove out of the station yard, Emery saw Mary Spivac sitting in the Spivac truck. She waved at him, but he didn't wave back. How could she talk with young Bunce after his old man had rejected her dad's milk just a couple of mornings ago?

He drove such thoughts out of his mind. They didn't get their milk rejected this morning anyhow, he told himself. But it might be sent back tomorrow morning or the morning after. They needed to do something about this uncertainty.

"Dad," he said, "you were a member of the old small dairymen's organization. Couldn't you get Percy Woods to come down here and start it up again?"

His father stared at the highway. "We'll wait and see what Nels Peterson does. I think things'll start happening pretty soon."

Chapter Four

THE ORGANIZER

That evening just as Emery finished pouring the mash into the feed boxes, David and Prince arrived with the cows from the lower pasture. The black and white Holsteins jostled into the alleyway, hoofs thudding and clicking on the cement as they hurried to their respective stanchions.

The two brothers met at the upper end of the barn and David said: "Hey, Em, I got an idea today. I'm going to Cornell when I finish high school and study biology."

"About time you were making up your mind to study

27

something," Emery cracked. Then he frowned, reminded of Del Bunce's big talk about going to Cornell.

Mr. Crane brought in the milking machines, and David remarked: "Bunce sent Joe Meaney's milk back yesterday. Willy told me at school today."

Emery and his father looked at the boy sharply, and Mr. Crane said: "Anything can happen now. Joe Meaney and Nels Peterson don't fool around when they get mad." Then he added: "Turn on the milker, Dave."

The boy pulled a switch and a motor began to whirr followed by the "huh-huh-huh" sound of the air exhaust as the suction began in the milker pipes. Emery tore a square of paper toweling from a roll on the wall, picked up a milking machine, and went to two of his three cows. They were both four-year-olds, with heavy udders and broad hips.

"Over, Tassel. Over, Star!" He pushed them apart, wiped their udders with the paper towel, then swung the gleaming milker between them and fitted the rubber suction tube to the nozzle in the pipe line above the stanchions. When he turned a valve a "tuck-tuck-tuck" sound began in the machine.

He unhooked one set of teat-cups and turned a small lever on the pulsator head. Instantly the "tuck-tuck" sound of suction moved into the teat-cups. He slipped the cups, one at a time, over each of Tassel's teats, each cup pulling itself into position with a sucking sound. Now the "tuck-tuck" changed to "tink-tuck, tink-tuck" as the pulsator maintained the pull and release of the vacuum in the cups on the cow's udder.

After a quick glance at the window in the milker head

to see the milk gushing into the can, Emery unhooked the second unit and attached the cups to Star. He straightened up, listened a moment to the music of the milking, then walked to the end of the barn for two milk pails, one to empty the machine into, the other to "strip" the cows into after the machine had milked all it could.

When he returned, he felt the udders of the two cows being milked, then shut off the pulsator. Swinging the full machine to the alleyway, he poured the white, frothy milk into the pails. Then he re-set the machine on his other cow. He had to keep one set of cups idle while his third cow was milked. At this point he always thought: "If I had four cows, now, I could keep both sets of cups busy."

At the end of the milking, nine cans stood in the alleyway, seven of them full, one half full, and Emery's can more than half full. The milk flood was increasing.

"With tomorrow morning's milking, I'll make more than a can this time," Emery boasted.

"Looks like it," agreed his father. "Hope Bunce doesn't decide it's our turn to get our milk rejected again."

They carried the cans over to the milkhouse while David freed the cows from the stanchions and drove them out to pasture. Emery's face was screwed up with a frown: if Bunce sent the milk back again, he'd—he'd do something. But he realized helplessly that there was nothing he could do.

That evening Mr. Muller brought over the bean agreement. Emery read it over: he had to produce the land and Muller produced the market for the beans. They would split the cost of seed, fertilizer, baskets, picking, and hauling, and divide the profits.

As Emery signed, Muller said to his father, "Maybe you'd better countersign it, Lou—Emery's not of age yet." Then he wished them good luck and drove off.

"He seems like a good guy for a big producer," remarked Emery, looking after Muller's departing car.

"Yes." Mr. Crane squinted a little. "Yes, he does."

Emery took the bean agreement into the house, feeling that it was insurance against further milk rejections, but a little later his worry about more milk trouble was revived when his father read aloud an item from the Sheltonville *News-Star*.

"Mr. Percy Woods of St. Lawrence County warned yesterday that if the milk dealers maintained their present attitude toward the producers there would be trouble in the milk shed before the season is over.

" 'It's the same old story,' he said. 'People in New York City aren't buying all the milk they want because the price is too high. The dealers want to keep the price up and the fluid sale down so that more can be processed into powdered milk, cheese, etc., to the dealers' advantage, and cut the price to the producer. If the price of fluid milk is cut, more milk can be sold to New York people and the dairy men can get the same price they're getting now.' "

"Mmm, that's bringing it out in the open," concluded Mr. Crane. Then he added: "This fellow Humbert, who's just bought the *News-Star*, is going to get himself into trouble with the dealers and the big producers if he isn't careful."

Mrs. Crane sighed. "I suppose we'll have to take a

price-cut. And I did so hope we could get running water put into the house this year."

"The year isn't over yet," replied Mr. Crane.

"Dad, do you think Nels Peterson and Joe Meaney will get Percy Woods to come down here?" asked Emery.

"I don't know. This is a tough spot. There are enough big dairymen to keep the A.D. going without us little fellows. We haven't a weapon to fight them with except the strike and they can ignore us. A lot of small dairymen around here would organize right now if Jim Lane said the word. But Jim's a marked man—the dealers almost ruined him before." Mr. Crane broke off.

Bets looked up from her homework, her brown eyes bright. "You know what—I'm going to be in a debate with Chuck Lane. We're debating Charlie Speer and Caroline Haar—'Resolved that Cooperatives are good for the Community.' We're on the affirmative."

"Thought you were going to be a nurse," said Emery.

"I like debating too."

"Yeah. When it's with Chuck."

She made a face at him across the table. They said no more about the threatening trouble in the milk shed that evening, but a couple of nights later they heard footsteps on the porch, and Chuck Lane stuck his head in the door, a grin pushing up each side of his thin face.

"Hi, folks."

He was greeted with a chorus of "Hellos."

"Came over to work on our debate, Bets," he explained.

"But we don't have to start until next week, Chuck."

"Never put things off." His eyes twinkled. "Besides, Nels Peterson and Joe Meaney are over talking to Dad, so I thought I'd come over here."

The Cranes were startled. This news could mean only one thing: the small producers were stirring into action.

Milk rejections continued at the A.D. station, but the Crane's milk was taken regularly. The milk flood continued to swell at the dairies. And the wild apples on the ridges turned pink with blossoms like sun-flushed snow; the oat field above the Crane house turned faintly green, a greenness that thickened and darkened and deepened day by day.

One morning Mr. Crane said to Emery: "Better come along with me to the station and help me get a load of cow feed."

At the station, Emery's father said: "You unload and pick up the empties. I want to get a loan at the office against my next month's milk check to pay for the feed."

While Emery waited for cans "77" at the end of the line, he noticed the Spivac pickup truck at the rear of the station and Jack Spivac filling cans with scalding water to take home. Young Bunce was talking to Mary in the cab. Emery looked away. I'll bet he talks to her every morning, he thought.

He saw Dan Jessup drive his truck up to the receiving end of the line. Harold Shontz pulled up behind him, leaned out of his cab, and yelled: "Hey, Dan, that organizer guy was up to my place last night. I took the shotgun to him. He cleared out fast." Shontz laughed loudly.

"I chased him off last week," Jessup yelled back.

Emery felt numb. So that was what had been happening. He saw young Bunce going toward the office, acting as if he hadn't heard what the two dairymen had said. Emery thought: That's the kind of talk his old man'll like to hear—his old man and the dealers.

While he and his father drove home with the load of cow feed, Emery remained glumly silent. He couldn't bring himself to tell his father what he'd overheard. When they passed the cheese factory in Atlas, he just said wistfully: "Gee, I wish that was running." Mr. Crane didn't reply.

That evening, after supper, a car drove into the yard, and a solidly built man of medium height got out and came briskly up to the house. It was Percy Woods of St. Lawrence County. His blue eyes were bright, vivid as cornflowers; his jaw was stubborn. When he removed his hat, a thick wing of cornstalk-colored hair fell back on the right side of his forehead.

"I've been expecting you, Percy," greeted Mr. Crane. "Tell us what's happening around here."

"Plenty, Lou. I'm grinning."

"Anybody signing up?"

"I'm grinning," Percy Woods repeated.

Emery remembered the conversation overheard at the station that morning and reported it.

Woods chuckled. "I expect you folks to chase me off with the shotgun too." His chuckle rose to a merry laugh.

Now Emery understood. The organization was trying to get solid before the A.D. got wise.

Later, all the Cranes followed Percy Woods out to his car, and Mr. Crane shouted. "Get off my farm and don't show up around here again, or I'll let you have both barrels." And Percy Woods slammed into his car and roared out of the yard.

"Hope somebody was spying and heard that," said Bets gleefully.

And Emery went to bed that night chuckling to himself.

Chapter Five

STRATEGY

During the next week, ten more dairymen had their milk rejected by the A.D. "Bunce must be crazy," Mr. Crane said, "he's making the small dairymen mad enough to strike."

That gave Emery a sinking feeling in the stomach. Out of their next milk check, he expected to get almost a hundred dollars. If a strike were called he wouldn't be earning money to buy more cows. But Emery hadn't much time to brood over this problem because he and his father were busy getting their corn ground ready for planting.

Then one evening at supper, Bets remarked: "We lost our debate, Chuck and I."

"Couldn't you two out-talk Caroline and Charlie on Co-ops?" Emery asked.

Bets sniffed. "Mr. Haley and Mr. Tate voted against us. As a banker and a lawyer they'd be against us no matter how well we argued our side, Chuck says. Only Mr. Humbert voted for us."

Her father looked up. "So Humbert voted for you. He must be pretty liberal for a newspaper editor."

That evening Jim Lane came over. His face was paler than a farmer's should be, but the Cranes knew that Jim's complexion had been fine before he spent six months in jail during the big milk strike years back.

He was a big man, admired by the small dairymen, although they avoided him in public. After that strike the A.D. had put a social quarantine on Jim Lane; if any farmer was seen talking to him, that farmer had his milk rejected as a warning. Of course it wasn't rejected openly for that reason—it was supposed to smell bad. But the dairymen knew the real reason and shunned Lane in public.

The A.D. had blacklisted Jim Lane's milk and Emery remembered that there were always two more cans of milk in their cooler every morning than they made themselves. His father took the extra cans to the A.D. with his. And the other neighbors of the Lanes did the same for them. It was only recently that the A.D. had taken Jim Lane back as a regular patron.

The Cranes greeted Jim noisily and Mr. Crane asked: "What's new, Jim?"

"We've got fifty-one dairymen signed up."

"That number could pull a real strike," said Mr. Crane.

"Maybe that's what the A.D. wants," replied Lane. "We might close the station, but the big producers could take the loss, while we little dairymen couldn't. The big fellows are gobbling up the little fellows all the time. There's MacKensie over at Atlas. He used to own his dairy, but he got in debt to the A.D. and Biggart, and now he runs the dairy just for the Biggart chain. A strike would weaken enough little producers so the big ones could pick 'em off."

A gloomy silence grew in the room. Emery realized that what Jim Lane had just said made sense: if Bunce continued rejecting milk, the small dairymen would get mad and strike, and a lot of them would go broke. But what else could they do? His mind searched frantically for an answer.

Mr. Crane said slowly: "Looks as if we need something bigger than the strike as a weapon to defend ourselves."

Jim Lane nodded.

Emery's searching mind stumbled: MacKensie near *Atlas*—Atlas meant *cheese factory*. Bets had lost her debate on Co-ops. He squirmed in his chair, then broke into the conversation: "Why couldn't we buy that cheese factory in Atlas and operate it as a co-operative?"

For a moment his father and Mr. Lane seemed not to have heard him. Then Mr. Crane said: "If the A.D. shut out the small producers there'd be more milk than that cheese factory could handle."

But Jim Lane spoke up. "Maybe you've got something, Emery! That cheese factory might be converted into a milk station—a Co-op milk station. We could sell to the Consumer Co-op in New York City just as the folks in St. Lawrence County do." He slapped his thighs excitedly. "What's in that factory? Any equipment?"

"Let's go have a look," Emery blurted out. "Maybe we can get in through a window—there's no watchman there."

Mr. Lane chuckled. "How about it, Lou? Why don't we give it a look?"

"Okay," said Mr. Crane. "If we could pull off such a deal, we'd really have the A.D. over a barrel."

Instantly the three of them were on their feet, pulling on their jackets. Emery's hand trembled with excitement as he slipped the flashlight into his pocket.

"We'd better walk," said his father. "You lead, Em. You know the way better than we do."

Down past the barn they went, and up over the east ridge to the quiet village of Atlas. When they reached the highway above the railroad station, they waited until no cars were in sight, then dashed across and down the tracks to the hulking shadow that was the cheese factory. Emery found a window with a pane of glass broken out.

"Dad, lift me up," he whispered. "Maybe we can unlock this window."

He felt strong arms lifting him up. When he reached the level of the gaping hole, he slipped his hand through and tugged at the rusted catch lever of the metal sash. It gave suddenly and the window swung free with a groan. His father let him down and the three listened. The village remained quiet.

"Lift me up again," Emery whispered. "I'm going in."

Again he was pushed up. He tilted the window and wriggled through. The flashlight in his pocket thumped against the sill. He heard Jim Lane whisper, "I'm coming, too." Then he and Emery reached down and pulled Mr. Crane in after them.

They waited, listening tensely; then Jim Lane said: "Let's see what's here."

"Turn on your flash, Em," ordered his father. "But hold your fingers over the light and keep it low."

The faint glow revealed a row of vats. They were in the cheese room. Off to the left were the presses, molds, and packaging machines. They moved cautiously toward a door standing ajar, and entered the main room. All the equipment was still there—the receiving platform, weighing machine, sterilizer, cooling machine, and two huge thousand-gallon storage tanks.

Without actually being able to see it, they knew that everything was covered with dust and grime. Their feet crunched on the fine coating of cinders on the floor as they walked.

They inspected each piece of equipment as well as they could in the faint light. Dark patches of rust showed up on the metal moorings. Off in the rear corner a door opened to a stairway down to the boiler room. Emery took his fingers off the light and flashed it briefly down the stairs. Rats stared at them, blinded by the light. Then he covered the beam again.

"Everything's here," whispered Jim Lane. "It could be fixed up and converted into a milk station."

"We've seen all we need to see," replied Mr. Crane.

Emery led the way back to the open window and they slipped out.

Silently, they headed up over the ridge again. Emery felt flushed and excited: if they could just buy that old plant and convert it, they'd have a way to fight the A.D. But neither his father nor Jim Lane spoke until they had reached the Crane's pasture and were almost home.

"I'd better get in touch with Percy Woods tomorrow," Jim Lane said. "If the organization here could get that cheese factory and form a co-operative—a real co-op, not a phoney—one vote to a shareholder, not one vote to a share—then we'd have a weapon stronger than the strike."

"Who owns that factory?" asked Mr. Crane.

After a pause, Jim Lane said: "The bank in Shelton-ville, I believe. That's my impression."

"The bank's a big stockholder in the A.D.," Mr. Crane pointed out. "They probably wouldn't sell it to us."

The three walked on in silence. Mr. Haley, president of the Sheltonville bank, had voted against Bets in her debate on Co-ops.

When they reached the yard, Jim Lane said: "I'll have a talk with Percy—maybe with some of the others. We ought to be able to find a way to swing it." Then he added: "I'd better get on home now." He strode off down the drive.

Emery followed his father up to the house. Bets and David were already in bed. His mother sat by the dining-room table, reading, and she looked up eagerly.

"What did you find out?" she asked.

"All the equipment's there," replied Mr. Crane. "But Jim thinks the bank owns it and they hold A.D. stock."

"They won't sell it then," predicted Mrs. Crane.

His mother's reiteration of the conclusion they had already reached seemed to rub in the fact that they were at a dead end. The scheme was washed up before it was even started.

"Guess I'll go to bed," he said. "Five o'clock isn't very far off."

Just before he fell asleep, his habit of thinking about the next day's work reminded him that in a few days he'd have to start getting that five acres of land ready for beans.

"Anyhow, I've got that bean deal," he muttered.

Maybe he'd be able to make enough from the beans to buy more cows. But that speculation brought the unhappy question: what was the good of getting more cows if he couldn't sell their milk? He turned over on his stomach with a grunt and stubbornly went to sleep.

Chapter Six

CANNING FACTORY

After that night they didn't see Jim Lane for a while and Emery wondered what was happening. Had the idea been given up? But the arrival of the milk check diverted his thoughts. His share was $96.34. With his savings, this gave him more than enough to buy a cow.

That afternoon while he and his father washed the walls of the dairy in preparation for a new coat of paint, he said: "Will you sell me that two-year-old that'll have a calf this October, Dad? The one we call Checkers?"

"Save your money," replied Mr. Crane. "Better think

up something sounder than dairy farming. Three more dairymen had their milk rejected this morning."

A fellow didn't have a chance, Emery thought miserably.

The next morning Emery took the milk to the station while his father started spraying paint on the dairy walls. When he stopped the truck at the receiving conveyor, Emery saw the Spivac pickup parked at the side of the yard. Emery wondered why Spivac seemed to have so much business here, then answered himself at once: who cares?

As he unloaded, he heard Mr. Bunce rejecting another dairy man's milk. He waited glumly in the truck for their empty cans at the other end of the conveyor line. A voice at the cab window surprised him.

"What's the matter, Em?"

It was Mary Spivac.

"Nothing," he answered rudely. "Nothing's the matter with me. Where's your fat boy friend?"

Her chin jerked as if he'd slapped her. "All right for you, Emery Crane!"

Her long legs in jeans, her squared shoulders, and the resolute poise of her head as she marched away stuck in his mind. He told himself that he didn't care—let her be mad.

On the way home Emery automatically glanced toward the old cheese factory when he drove through Atlas. A car was parked in the yard and a group of men were going over the property. Who was that? Was someone going to buy the plant? He pressed harder on the gas pedal and the truck roared furiously on toward home.

Mr. Crane received the news soberly: "Maybe some-body's getting interested in it."

"If somebody else buys it, we're sunk, Dad," Emery cried.

"Maybe we are buying it," replied his father.

That gave Emery something to think about. As he plowed the five-acre field for beans that afternoon, he was filled with new hope.

At milking time, David and Prince drove up a broad-hipped Holstein they called Square-head and her new knockkneed black-and-white calf. This reminded Emery of his hope of buying another cow and he again broached the subject to his father.

"Hold on to your money," Mr. Crane told him. "I'll need all the cows I've got and I'll be borrowing your money too, come September, to meet our obligations if the dealers push through a price-cut on us."

"But the cheese factory, Dad . . ."

"We don't know anything about the cheese factory."

The following afternoon, just as Emery was finishing disking in the fertilizer for the five acres of beans, Mr. Muller brought over the bean seed.

"Good news for us, Emery," he said. "I hear the old cheese factory's been sold for a canning factory. Now if we get stuck with some beans we can't ship to the New York market we can have them custom-packed at this cannery."

Emery felt as if he'd been kicked in the stomach, but he managed to grin feebly, then mumble: "Ye—yeah, good news."

After Muller left, he resumed his job, thinking: "We've lost our one chance to fight the A.D. Our one chance."

The cow Square-head and her new calf had been left in the barn all day and when Emery poured feed in her box that evening he noticed that she was fighting the stanchion, trying to get her head around to her flank. Her agate eyes were glazed. He felt his throat tighten with fear; she was sick.

His father wasn't in from planting corn yet, and David had gone for the other cows. He needed help. As he ran toward the milkhouse, he saw his sister feeding the chickens and yelled: "Bets! Come help me! Square-head's got milk fever."

They hadn't had a case of milk fever for several years and he pulled the air pump and tubes from the medicine chest in the milkhouse hoping they'd still be usable.

Bets met him at the milkhouse door. "Here, give me those," she ordered. "They've got to be sterilized."

She took the contraption out of his hands, kicked a pail under the hot water tap, then poured cleaning compound into it and turned on the water. Emery realized that his sister wasn't kidding when she talked about being a nurse.

"Is this all you need?" she asked.

"We need some cotton for the glass tube and adhesive tape to keep the air in the udder."

"You get them. Be sure you keep them clean."

She put the sterilized equipment in one pail and filled another with warm water. When they got back to the barn Emery freed the cow from the stanchion. He placed a bag of feed behind her shoulder so that she couldn't get over flat on her side.

"Poor Square-head," said Bets sympathetically. Then she began to wash the heavy, swollen udder thoroughly.

Spurred by his sister's carefulness, Emery washed and dried his hands before stuffing the cotton into the glass tube. He fixed one end of the glass to the pump hose, the other end to a rubber tube, and laid them across the top of the one pail. Bets dried the cow's udder, cut four squares of adhesive tape and stuck the corners to the rim of the metal bucket.

"You ready?" he asked.

"Ready," she replied.

The way she said it reminded him of the radio programs about doctors which she was always listening to.

"Tube," he said.

"Tube." She handed him the rubber tube and he fitted the end over the tiny opening in a lower teat.

"Pump."

"Pump." She began pumping slowly, inflating a quarter of the udder. The skin ballooned tight.

"Tape."

"Tape." She handed him a square of adhesive.

Pinching the end of the teat so that the air couldn't escape, he removed the tube and pressed tape over the teat opening to hold in the air. They repeated the treatment on the other three teats.

"Guess that ought to fix her up," Emery said.

Bets straightened up and seemed to mentally remove rubber gloves before she looked at the cow and murmured: "Poor old Square-head."

Mr. Crane came in from the field and examined the sick cow. "First-class piece of veterinary work," he told Emery and Bets. "You took care of her all right."

Bets' face glowed with pleasure.

And David teased: "At last our Florence Nightingale's found something to nurse."

Her bright eyes glared at him as she raised her hand for a good slap, but he took refuge among the cows.

During the milking, Emery remembered the canning factory deal and grumbled bitterly to himself: "Gee, what's the use trying to save a cow? Might as well lose 'em all, for all the chance small dairies like theirs had these days." But he didn't mention the news to his father.

After supper that evening, Percy Woods stopped in.

"What's the news of the Co-op?" Mr. Crane asked.

"That's what I came to talk about." Woods' blue eyes twinkled behind his glasses.

"But somebody's bought the cheese factory for a canning factory," Emery interrupted.

"That's right," said Woods. "But will you folks buy shares in a Co-op Milk Station?"

"Guess I can raise the money," replied Mr. Crane.

Emery couldn't follow this talk. "Mr. Muller said it was going to be a canning factory," he insisted.

"We bought it ostensibly for a canning factory," Woods explained, "because we knew the bank wouldn't sell it for a milk station. Our buyer let a hint drop that the place might be used in the off-season for a cheese factory. Even that worried them and they wrote a clause into the purchase agreement stating that we couldn't use it as a cheese factory. But they didn't say we couldn't use it as a milk station."

Emery understood now: they'd outsmarted the bank.

Percy Woods continued: "I'm making the rounds to see how many members can buy shares in the Co-op. Then I think we should have a public meeting. That won't surprise the A.D. They've been trying to stir up a strike."

Mr. Crane laced his fingers together. "A Co-op'll sure give the A.D. a jolt." He chuckled.

"Gee," Emery whispered, "I wish I could buy some shares in our Co-op."

Chapter Seven

SHAREHOLDER

A week of hot weather sent the young corn spearing up through the soft ground, and Emery's beans cracked the soil, bending pale stems into the light, shaking free green leaves. Summer had come to the ridges, valleys, wood lots, pastures, and fields of central New York State. The sun heat seemed to affect more than the land and the natural seed; it stirred the small dairy farmers and swelled the seed of the co-operative idea planted in the community.

"More than forty have signed for shares in the Co-op," Chuck Lane told Emery when they talked across the line fence, resting from cultivating corn. That news sent Emery back to work whistling.

One evening Jim Lane came over to ask Mr. Crane to go to the City with him in the morning on Co-op business. So Emery had to deliver the milk at the station.

When he pulled the truck in to unload, Homer Carsen's horse-drawn spring-wagon stood just outside the A.D. office. The gray horse, Sparks, dozed in the shafts. He had hauled Carsen's milk to the station for thirteen years; he could have brought it without anyone driving him.

Emery watched Homer Carsen drag a can of rejected milk out of the office. The old farmer's face was almost purple as he heaved the can into the spring-wagon.

Mr. Bunce appeared at the office door and glared at the dairymen waiting in the yard. "I hear a lot of you fellows have been organizing. Well, maybe your organization will take your rotten milk, but the Associated Dairymen won't."

"My milk ain't rotten," old Carsen yelled back. "It's as good as anything Biggart or Howells makes—better, by gum! I ain't never joined a organization, you fatheaded toad, but by gum, I'm goin' to belong and mighty quick." He clucked angrily to Sparks and drove off.

The dairymen smiled slyly; some even chuckled. Emery drove over to wait for the empty cans: that was the first time he'd ever known Homer Carsen to have his milk rejected. Bunce was pushing things mighty far. He noticed the Spivac truck parked at the rear of the station, and Mary was in the cab. On an impulse Emery went over to her.

"Hi, Mary," he greeted; then he felt embarrassed. "I didn't mean to get so thick the other morning. I'm sorry."

"You were jealous." She smiled, her eyes bright.

"I wasn't either. Where's your boy friend today?"

"Tending his beans." She continued to smile.

He knew she was teasing him. "What do you see in Fatso Bunce anyhow?"

"Lots." She laughed. "He's got twenty acres of beans. He's going to Cornell to learn how to tell you and my dad and yours how to run a dairy. He's going to get a car in a couple of weeks . . ."

"Well, if that's what you want . . ."

"And if I keep on talking to him he'll keep his dad from rejecting our milk," she finished.

Emery felt his face burning. "Oh—ah—"

"Let's change the subject. Dad says George Kressel has two heifers he wants to sell." Then Mary whispered: "He wants to raise the money to buy Co-op shares."

Emery lowered his voice. "I'd like to buy some shares too, but I can't buy Co-op and cows at the same time."

"Dad's borrowing from Muller on his beans to buy shares." Mary looked scared. "Don't you say anything; Muller doesn't know it."

"I sure won't," Emery said.

A dairyman yelled: "Hey, Emery, get your empties."

Emery loaded cans "77" on the truck and thought about what Mary had told him: suppose he borrowed five hundred dollars from Muller against his beans and bought Kressel's two heifers. Then he could use his savings to buy Co-op stock and Kressel could buy Co-op too. But

what if his beans didn't make a crop? Well, Jack Spivac
expected a crop; why shouldn't he?

That afternoon Mr. Muller dropped in to have a look
at the bean field. "You'll get a bumper crop, Emery, and
we'll have a big market this year." Then he changed the
subject. "Added any cows to your herd lately, Emery?"

"No sir." Then Emery added eagerly, "But I know of
a couple of good heifers I can buy."

"I like to see young fellows get a start," said Mr.
Muller. "I'll lend you money on those beans if you want
to get those heifers before someone else does."

"Gee, that'd be swell, Mr. Muller," exclaimed Emery.
"But it might take almost five hundred."

"Your beans'll back such a loan, son." Muller pulled
a promissory note blank from his pocket and began filling
it out. "Get your father's signature on this, too," he said
handing it to Emery. "Just a precaution, you know, because you're not of age; then bring it over to my office and
I'll give you a check for the money." He drove out of the
yard.

Emery's hands trembled with excitement as he read:
"Five hundred dollars to be repaid on or before August
15."

Mr. Crane came home from New York City that evening full of good news. "Everything's set. We'll call a
public meeting next week and organize the Co-op."

Before going to bed, Emery showed his father Muller's
note. Mr. Crane shook his head: "We don't know if you'll
get a crop or if Muller can sell them. And if I sign that
note, I'll have to make it good if you can't."

"But I'll get a crop, Dad, and there'll be a good market," Emery insisted. "I want those two heifers and I want to buy Co-op stock."

"I'll have to think it over, Em," replied Mr. Crane.

Several days passed, but his father didn't reach a decision. Emery grew impatient. Mr. Crane, Jim Lane, and Nels Peterson had been calling on the small dairymen, urging them to come to the big meeting the following Saturday night and getting promises of Co-op stock purchases. But Thursday night Mr. Crane came home looking tired and sober.

"Where's that note Muller gave you, Em?" he asked. "We've got to take a few chances. If you get this loan, that'll mean you and Kressel will become Co-op stockholders. It's risky," he slapped the note, "but I'll sign it."

The next morning when Emery took the milk to the station, he stopped at Muller's office on the way.

"Thought you didn't want those heifers," said Muller with a laugh. Then he wrote out a check. The amount read: "Four hundred and ninety-five dollars." He explained: "I've just deducted the interest in advance."

Emery hesitated, then took the check. This trick of deducting the interest in advance made him wonder: maybe Muller wasn't such a good guy after all. He deposited the money at the bank in Sheltonville, then drove over to George Kressel's.

Kressel, a tall farmer, straight and thin, took him out to the pasture and pointed out the two heifers. Emery looked them over carefully—broad hips, straight backs, straight necks. The metal clips in their ears indicated that they had been t.b. tested. He made them walk and examined their hoofs. Their bags looked as though they would make good milkers when they freshened.

He bought the pair for a hundred and seventy-five dollars each. That evening he and David drove them home. As they passed the Spivac place, Emery saw Mary and waved and she waved back. He thought, I'll see her at the meeting tomorrow night at Jim Lane's.

The Lane yard filled up with cars that Saturday night. The dairymen and their families crowded into the big dairy barn. Emery and Bets and Mary Spivac and Chuck Lane and the other young folks sat on the hayloft stairway and listened to the meeting.

Mr. Crane acted as chairman and called the crowd to order. Jim Lane explained the Co-op plan. Most of them had heard it before, he told the crowd, but he wanted to make sure they had it straight. "Ours must be a true Co-op," he said, "not a phoney. One vote for each shareholder, not one vote for each share, and each shareholder must be a milk producer."

The shares of stock were to sell for one hundred dollars and could be sold back to the Co-op at par value any time the owner wished, payment being made within sixty days. The Co-op station would pay the regular price per hundredweight for milk, but five cents on every dollar would be deducted to pay for the station. However, in the sale and handling of the fluid milk, any profit would be returned to the stockholders in the form of dividends. The Consumers Cooperative in New York City would buy their milk.

Then Mr. Crane asked the dairymen to pledge the

number of shares they'd be ready to buy when called upon. The men began moving forward to put down their names.

Emery sat still, letting the others go, and Mary whispered: "Aren't you going up, Em?"

"Sure," he said, "but there's no hurry." It was pleasant to sit there and think: now I have five cows and we'll have a milk station belonging to all of us, and I'll be a patron. Finally he joined the end of the line of signers, wrote his name after Hans Overgaard's and put the number "3" for shares after it; then he swaggered back to the hayloft stairway.

"Dairyman Crane," Mary said, smiling at him.

He felt wonderful.

After a tally of promised shares, Mr. Crane announced: "We've the promise of a hundred and fifty-three shares, more than fifteen thousand dollars." The crowd applauded loudly. "That'll swing the deal and give us working capital."

Nominations were made for the board of directors. Jim Lane was elected chairman of the board, and the other six members were: Jack Spivac, Lou Crane, Mike Hollis, Homer Carsen, Charlie Bullock and Nels Peterson. The board was directed to complete the Co-op organization, get it chartered, incorporated, and begin operating the station.

Just before they adjourned, Percy Woods addressed the crowd: "I want to warn all of you: after tonight, the fat's in the fire and the A.D. will try to break you. They can't reject your milk entirely if it passes inspection. They can't lock you out. But they'll pull every trick in the bag against you while you still have to deliver your milk to them before your own station gets into operation. The A.D.'s been hoping you'd strike. They're not going to like what you're doing instead. So remember, be on your guard, or you'll lose before you've started. Now congratulations and good luck."

The crowd cheered him; then surged out on the Lane's lawn to eat sandwiches, cake, and ice cream and drink coffee and chocolate milk. Mary and Emery and Bets and Chuck sat on the steps of the Lane porch to eat. The moon was high and bright above them. Their faces were eager in the light.

"Won't it be wonderful when we don't have to take our milk to the A.D. any more?" said Mary happily. "Won't it?"

"I'll break down and cry." Chuck laughed.

"We've got a chance now," spoke up Emery. "I mean we kids have. Next year if I can get three more cows maybe I can rent the old Armstrong place and start dairying on my own."

"Now that I'm through high school," Chuck said, "I'm going to start building a herd of my own."

Then Bets brought out her dream too. "I'm going to Utica this fall to study nursing," she said. "And Miss Prentis, the county nurse, says I can go out with her sometimes this summer, if Mother will let me."

Only Mary seemed troubled by the future. "I wonder what Mr. Bunce will do when he hears about tonight," she said.

"He'll try something, that's for sure," muttered Emery.

They all grew silent, realizing that there might be trouble ahead.

Chapter Eight

TROUBLE

After that meeting Mr. Crane worked at Co-op organization, and the responsibility for running the dairy rested
upon Emery. Every morning when he delivered the milk
at the A.D. Station he expected trouble. But three days
passed and nothing happened. One evening, after supper,
he picked up the Sheltonville *News-Star*.

A front-page story caught his attention: "CO-OP FOR
ATLAS." He read it quickly. All the details were there:
the directors' names, and the plans for converting the
cheese factory into a milk station. Inside the paper an
editorial was headed, "WE NEED MORE CO-OPS." Mr.

Humbert argued that for the small dairymen to survive
they had to take the disposal of their milk out of the
hands of the big dealers and sell it themselves.

"Whew!" Emery exclaimed. "Wait till Dad sees that."

"Wait till Mr. Bunce sees it," said his mother soberly.

When Emery hauled the milk to the station in the
morning, his mouth felt dry: maybe all the little dairymen would have their milk rejected. But the only unusual
thing he noticed was the presence of the big producers'
cars. The big shots were apparently in a huddle with
Bunce. The meeting ended before Emery could pick up
his empties and get away, and Mr. Muller, seeing him,
came over to his truck.

"Morning, Emery," he said. "So you folks are starting a
Co-op. I've been warning Bunce all spring that he was
being too rough on the small producers."

Emery was surprised at Muller's friendly tone. "It
seemed like the only chance we had," he answered.

"You might be doing the right thing," Muller continued. "Might even join you myself. But I don't like
your vote ruling—it should be a vote per share."

"That'd make it too easy for one person to get control of the whole organization," Emery explained quickly.

"It's like this, son," Muller said. "Suppose you work
harder than I do and you're smarter, and you can buy
ten shares, while I buy only one. When it comes to voting,
I'm just as good as you. That isn't right. That isn't American; it isn't the way this country was built. The smarter
and harder working a fellow is, the more to his credit
and the more power he's a right to. Isn't that so?"

Emery was silent. He knew all these arguments.

"Think it over, son," Muller advised. Then he added: "How're the beans?"

"Blossoming. They're full."

"I'll be getting my niggers any day now."

Emery strangled a sudden bitter anger: Muller spoke of his seasonal labor gang as if they were slaves. The big dairyman's parting advice was, "Don't forget, son, if you don't fight for a vote a share in that Co-op, they'll make a sucker out of you."

As Emery drove home he kept wondering about Muller's attitude, wondering what had been decided at the big-producers' meeting. That noon he reported what had happened at the station, mentioning also the expected arrival of Muller's labor gang.

Bets spoke up: "Miss Prentis says she's going to make him give those Negroes better places to live in. The County doesn't want her to because it's run by the big producers but she told them straight out that those shacks were a menace to the public health. She's a real fighter, Miss Prentis is. That's why I want to help her this summer."

Her mother looked worried. "You might catch some awful disease going among those poor people, Bets."

"But, Mother," the girl protested, "I'm going to study to be a nurse. If Miss Prentis isn't afraid to help those people, I'm not." Then she added as an afterthought: "Mr. Humbert's supporting her clean-up program."

That afternoon on the way to the hayfield, it occurred to Emery that if Bets got mixed up in pressure to clean up Muller's shack colony, the big dairyman might try to get even by making trouble over the beans, or the five hundred dollars Emery owed him. Bets ought to stay out of that business, he thought, but immediately felt ashamed of himself for his selfishness.

Mr. Crane got home at milking time and came down to the barn, grinning broadly. "How're you kids making out?"

"Okay," Emery replied. "How're *you* making out?"

"We're ready to take your money."

After supper, Emery wrote out a check to the Co-op and his father gave him a certificate for three shares— crisp paper with wavy green lines, and a green circle around two evergreen trees. Emery fingered it proudly.

The next morning when he delivered the milk, Mr. Bunce was out talking to the various dairymen and came over to his truck. "Morning, Em, how's the new Co-op?"

Emery felt his spine tingle. "Fine, sir, I guess."

"For your information," Bunce continued with a satisfied grin, "the A.D. plans to remove part of the equipment here as soon as you fellows pull out. We'll cut down the amount of milk we can handle to just the number of patrons who stay with us. So when your little venture flops, you won't be able to get back in here. Think it over."

"In that case, sir," Emery replied slowly, "it looks as if we won't dare flop."

Mr. Bunce walked away without replying.

That evening Mr. Crane came home, looking tired and worried, reporting that three dairymen had pulled out without giving any reasons. Emery told him about Bunce's threat and his father nodded, understanding. The fight was on. Later, another dairyman called up and wanted to sell back his stock. Emery overheard his father's half of the conversation. Mr. Crane told the man they would buy back his shares at the end of the sixty-day period specified, but he hoped he would reconsider.

Then Mr. Crane drove over to see Jim Lane, and Emery went to bed worrying. At milking time the next morning, the only news he could get out of his father was the plan for another meeting this coming Saturday night. Mr. Crane refused to tell him how many had withdrawn.

After breakfast Emery glumly drove their load of milk down to the station. When he stopped at the receiving end, he saw the Spivac truck at the other end and Del Bunce was helping Mary load on the empties. She had been delivering their milk since Jack Spivac had become busy with the Co-op organization. Young Bunce seemed to be having a lot to say to her.

Emery tried to ignore them. As his last can slid through the swinging door onto the receiving platform, the door stayed open and one of the handlers stuck his head out of the opening.

"Hey," he called to Emery, "you a Co-op? Hope you choke. You rats are takin' my job away from me. When you quit haulin', I'm fired. Hope you choke!" The door slammed shut.

The man's anger startled Emery. He realized that when the Co-op members pulled out of the A.D. some of the station help would be laid off. These men could be made to hate the Co-op. He climbed down into his truck cab.

Del Bunce, heading for the office, yelled to him: "Hi, Crane. You guys wised up yet that your coop's goin' boop and you'll be in the soup?" He laughed loudly.

"Anyhow, we won't be the A.D.'s dupe," Emery retorted.

Then he saw Mary driving out of the yard. On the way home, he came up with her parked on the roadside west of Sheltonville. She signalled him to stop. He thought she must be having car trouble, but the moment he got out of his truck, she began talking rapidly.

"Buncey told me this morning to tell my dad that if we'd pull out of the Co-op the A.D. would see that we got a better butterfat rating."

"But your dad won't fall for that," he replied quickly.

She hesitated a moment. "No, of course he won't." Then she added: "But I'm not going to tell him." She gave Emery an appealing look. "Dad's terribly in debt to the A.D., and the bank, and now to Muller. He figured that if the Co-op worked he'd have a chance of paying off his debts and being free again. But they're after him from all sides. They want to take over our dairy."

"Your dad's one of the directors," Emery pointed out. "If he pulls out of the Co-op a lot of the others will go with him."

"That's what I'm afraid of," Mary said. "Dad won't want to pull out, but he's cornered. That's why I won't tell him what Buncey said. I don't want to tempt him. We can't let the Co-op fall apart."

"It's got to work." Emery slowly shook his head. "We'll have to see what happens at the next meeting."

The crowd wasn't as big on Saturday night as it had

been at the first meeting. Jim Lane gave a report on progress: they had enough stock sold to take over possession of the cheese factory. This news was greeted by a mild cheer. Then he recounted the A.D.'s lock-out threat and the butterfat bribe.

"Suppose the A.D. does reduce their equipment so they can't take us back if the Co-op fails," he said. "There can be only one answer to that: we're not going to fail. Some of you have been offered more butterfat to pull out of the Co-op. Where is the A.D. going to get that butterfat? From the big producers, of course. And if the A.D. licks us, do you think the big producers will continue to let you have that edge on butterfat? You'll take a cut then to repay the big fellows."

The crowd murmured sullenly. At this point Jim Lane turned the meeting over to Percy Woods. Emery and Mary were sitting along the stanchion butt listening. When Mr. Lane had talked about the butterfat bribe, Emery was careful not to look at Mary. Yet he had a feeling of frustration which made him fidget.

Percy Woods told the crowd the number of small dairies in the county that had been taken over by the big dairymen during the past year. That was the threat which faced every dairyman present here tonight, he pointed out. And the only possible way for them to save themselves was by building the Co-op.

Emery brightened up: that was telling them straight.

"The Sheltonville Bank," Woods shouted, "will be glad to buy the cheese factory back and remove the Co-op threat. You can get your money back now and call the whole thing off."

His voice rose angrily. "You can wreck your chances of keeping your dairies! You can keep your kids from ever being independent dairymen! You can wash out the Co-op and crawl back to the A.D." His blue eyes blazed. "Is that what you small dairymen want to do?"

Silence, deep and tense, followed the question. Emery felt his body quivering all over; then he sprang to his feet and yelled: "NO! We want the Co-op!"

Across the barn, Joe Meaney yelled back: "We want the Co-op!" Others took up the yell.

Jim Lane brought order again. Almost at once, Jack Spivac moved that the board of directors be ordered to take possession of the old cheese factory on Monday. The motion was seconded by a chorus of voices, Emery's one of them, and it was carried by a shout of approval.

Then Emery looked around at Mary. She was smiling, holding out her hand. He took it and they shook as if sealing a bargain, and both laughed happily.

"I guess the Co-op's over one bump," he said, with a sigh of satisfaction.

Chapter Nine

PASSING INSPECTION

Emery was in the first gang of Co-op members who turned out Monday morning to begin cleaning up the old cheese factory. He saw smoke pouring from the boiler-room chimney when he arrived. Sam Rudnek, a stocky man with bushy gray hair, fierce eyebrows and a very red face, had been hired to manage the station. He and Jim Lane and several others were already there.

"You're the boss here, Sam," Lane told him. "We're expecting you to get this place past inspection, so give the orders and we'll carry 'em out."

"It's going to be tough." Sam shook his bushy head.

"The A.D. crowd will have a hand on every one of the three inspectors, so this place'll have to be better than perfect."

Emery helped sweep the plant and carry the accumulated rubbish out and burn it. By the time that job was finished, steam pressure was up and he and Harold Shontz went over the ceiling, walls, and floor with the steam hose, gouging out every crack, corner, and crevice with steam.

Three of the men began spraying a coat of white paint on the outside of the building, and Hans Overgaard glazed the broken windows. By evening the cheese factory stood in the dark cinder yard like a white monument. Emery and the other members proudly surveyed their day's work.

"We did all right, gentlemen," said Mr. Rudnek, his red face beaming. "By afternoon tomorrow the next crew can start spraying the paint on the inside." He turned to Jim Lane. "Send around your best mechanics, Jim. We've got to take down every piece of equipment and re-condition it."

Lane nodded, adding: "Drop over this evening, Sam."

"Thanks, I'd like to." Rudnek frowned. "But I guess I'd better stay here. This is my responsibility; I want to see it through inspection and I don't want anything to happen to it."

Jim Lane took Emery home. When he got out at their drive, Emery said: "Do you think it's all right to leave Mr. Rudnek at the station alone?"

The tall dairyman frowned. "I don't think the A.D.

gang would dare to do anything to the place, but you can't ever tell." He laughed nervously. "How about you and Chuck going down?"

"I'll be glad to go," agreed Emery eagerly.

When Emery reported this at supper, Mr. Crane said: "They wouldn't dare to try any tricks . . ." He broke off, then added, "Or would they?"

Emery and Chuck walked over the ridge to the cheese factory and Sam was glad to see them. "I didn't want to ask for anybody," he admitted. "But I couldn't stay awake all night and be any good tomorrow."

The three sat in the office talking in low tones. Sam told the boys about a Co-op station he had managed up in St. Lawrence County which the big producers had tried to wreck. They'd tried all sorts of tricks but they'd failed.

At ten o'clock Chuck and Sam stretched out on the office floor to sleep while Emery stood the first watch. He felt keyed up, expecting trouble, but nothing happened. At one o'clock he woke Chuck and stretched out to sleep himself. In the morning, after Sam's watch, all three felt a little foolish and told each other that the A.D. gang wouldn't dare do anything to their Co-op station.

The next day another crew took over the work on the cheese factory and Emery helped his father make hay. But after supper he decided to walk over to Atlas to see what progress had been made, and maybe to stay all night again.

At ten o'clock Sam went to bed and Emery again took the first watch. Nothing had happened the night before and he felt that nothing was going to happen tonight either. He relaxed comfortably in a chair leaning back against the receiving platform.

The next thing he knew he was dreaming that someone was outside his bedroom window sawing wood. Suddenly he was awake. Somewhere beyond the first storage tank was the sound of scraping. A feeling of terror froze him for a moment; then he tiptoed across the floor to the edge of the tank and peered past it into the darkness.

His eyes searched the row of windows. Just back of one pane of glass he could make out movement, a darker shadow moving in a shadow. The scraping stopped and he heard a prying noise. Suddenly, as he strained his eyes harder to see, he realized that one of the panes of glass had been removed.

He ducked back toward the office intending to awaken Sam. Then he changed his mind. Maybe there wasn't time; maybe he ought to collar the prowler and yell for Sam. He crept over to the station door, opened it, and moved silently along the end of the building.

From the darkness some distance away came a low whistle. Emery leaped around the corner yelling for Sam. He saw a stocky figure disappearing in the darkness, running with a waddling gait. Emery didn't follow him beyond the edge of the station yard. When he came back, Sam was outside, waiting for him, flashlight blazing.

"Somebody took out a pane of glass," Emery panted and showed Sam the window. On the ground he noticed a white cylinder. "Looks as if he dropped a cigarette too." He stooped to pick it up. "This isn't a cigarette," he said.

Sam turned the flashlight and they saw the end of a dynamite fuse. One tip was damp, indicating that it had probably been carelessly carried through dew-wet bushes and this end had had to be cut off to get at dry powder.

"By golly!" Sam exclaimed. "They were trying to blow us up. We'd better call the troopers."

They returned to the office and Sam called the police. When they arrived, the sergeant in command examined the gaping window and the fuse end and said: "I don't think they'll be back, but I'll station a man here until morning."

At breakfast Emery told the family what had happened.

After a startled silence, Mr. Crane said: "Well, you can see what we're up against. They'll stop at nothing."

When Emery took the milk to the A.D. Station the story was already buzzing among the dairymen present. They crowded around Emery asking questions. Manager Bunce saw an opportunity to lash out at the Co-op dairymen and flung open the window by the receiving platform.

"What happened last night shows you're licked already," he bawled. "It was Lane who tried to blow up that old cheese factory so's you wouldn't have to open the place and fail like you're going to."

Nels Peterson yelled back sarcastically: "You'd hate it, wouldn't you Bunce, if we failed."

Emery saw the handler who had complained to him about the Co-op making him lose his job, walking along the receiving platform behind the manager. The handler's bow-legged gait caught Emery's attention. He had a feeling that it should mean something to him.

A thorough police checkup revealed nothing new in the cheese factory incident and the community was left to speculate and surmise. Bunce's version of what had been intended was listened to by some and grew in the retelling. It was said that the Co-op directors had attempted to blow up the new plant and abscond with the members' money. Some of the Co-op members believed it. Nick Shostikov wanted to sell back his stock and pull out.

Mr. Crane bristled: "Okay. In sixty days you can have your money. By that time we'll be in operation—and you won't get back into the Co-op again when the A.D. starts rejecting your milk and cutting your butterfat rating."

Shostikov walked away and left Mr. Crane looking worried. But Emery, who had overheard, said: "That's tellin' him, Dad. It's time we stopped babying these weak sisters."

"Maybe I shouldn't have told him off," his father answered. "But they get in my back hair sometimes."

Inspection was set for Saturday afternoon and the station would be ready, but Friday, when Emery took the milk to the A.D., he saw Del Bunce for the first time in a week. He drove a new convertible up to the office and got out.

"Think your coopity-boop will pass inspection, Crane?" he yelled jeeringly.

"Easily," Emery retorted, "if we get honest inspection."

"Honest!" Young Bunce guffawed. "You mean if you can buy them." Then he said loudly, "Maybe you guys don't want to pass inspection—that would be a nice out for your sure failure."

Emery didn't answer. Such an idea could be built into a backfire by the big producers against the possibility that the inspectors would be tough and the A.D. would be accused of paying them for not passing the Co-op station. He felt a sudden chill, realizing that their plant might not be approved.

They simply had to make sure of a fair inspection, he told himself. But how? No plan came to him.

That noon his sister remarked: "Did you see any of the Negro field help at Muller's?" He remembered having noticed some activity back among Muller's shacks, but he hadn't thought about it. Bets continued: "There was a story in yesterday's *News-Star* about them, and Mr. Humbert ran an editorial about the condition of those shacks."

Emery didn't say anything, but he was reminded of his beans. In a few days they'd be ready for the first picking. He tried to keep his mind off the coming inspection, but that evening Jim Lane stopped in and said: "I guess we're as ready as we'll ever be. It's going to be a tough inspection though."

In the morning, Emery saw Mary at the A.D.

"Today's the day," she said excitedly.

"Maybe the dice are loaded," he replied glumly.

"I hope not." A frown wrinkled her forehead. "If there were just somebody on our side who could expose the inspection if it wasn't fair."

Emery remembered the editorial in the *News-Star* about the living conditions of the migrant colored workers employed by the big dairymen. His memory went back farther: Mr. Humbert had once run an editorial in favor of Co-ops.

"See you at the inspection this afternoon," he said to Mary and walked hurriedly away.

On the way home he stopped in Sheltonville and went to the newspaper office. Mr. Humbert, a tall, lean young man with sharp gray eyes and a stubborn chin, asked briskly, "What can I do for you?"

"Well—I—liked your editorial about Co-ops awhile back, and I—wondered if you were—maybe on our side."

"I'm on the side that plays fair. What's your problem?"

Emery told him about the coming inspection and the fear that the inspectors might be paid for refusing to pass the new station.

"Nonsense!" snapped Mr. Humbert. "Our health inspectors can't be bribed. If the Co-op station is passable, it'll be passed." His sharp eyes never flickered from Emery's face. "What time is the inspection?"

"Three o'clock."

Emery left with an empty feeling in his stomach. No help there; the Co-op would just have to take its chances.

A crowd had gathered at the Co-op station by the time the three inspectors arrived. Emery and Mary saw them nod to Jim Lane and Sam Rudnek and begin their inspection. After a quick glance at the outside of the building, one of them remarked: "It needs a coat of paint." Another of the inspectors, carrying a clipboard holding paper, made a note of this.

Emery knew that the station had been given three coats of paint and he thought: if this is how it's starting, we haven't a chance. Just then Mr. Humbert arrived. He came breezily through the crowd and introduced himself to the inspectors: "I'm the editor of the *News-Star* and a local correspondent for the Associated Press."

"There's no story here," replied one of the inspectors gruffly.

"I believe there is." Mr. Humbert smiled pleasantly. "I've heard a number of nasty stories to the effect that you gentlemen have been bought off by the Associated Dairymen so that you won't pass this new station." He was careful to speak loud enough for the whole crowd to hear him. "I'd like to go along with you so that I can report a fair inspection."

The inspectors glared angrily around; then one of them growled: "Well, come along and see for yourself."

Emery noticed the man with the clipboard pause and cross out the notation that the station needed a coat of paint.

Half an hour later, the inspectors, Jim Lane, Sam Rudnek, and Mr. Humbert returned to the front of the station. All six of them seemed on friendly terms now. The spokesman for the inspectors addressed the crowd: "You've a fine station. We'll okay your opening Monday morning."

A spontaneous cheer went up from the crowd of Co-op members.

Mary clutched Emery's arm. "Isn't that swell, Em?"

"Sure is." He felt like yelling. His glance rose to the

big sign: ATLAS DAIRIES CO-OP, INC. There it was; it was real. They'd be bringing their milk here Monday. He glanced around quickly for Mr. Humbert but the editor had already driven away. The crowd was breaking up and going home to evening chores.

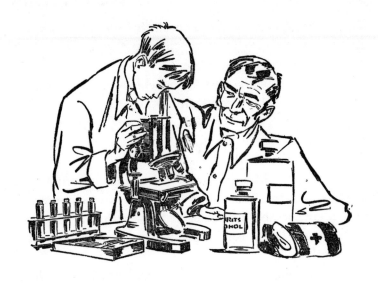

Chapter Ten

THE OPENING

The sky was a bright glow in the east on Monday morning when Emery went for the cows. He knew where the sun would soon notch the horizon and just below that notch was Atlas, and in Atlas was the new Co-op station, and today was the opening.

This morning he'd have his own cans—number "18." He was a Co-op patron, making more than a can and a half a day. That was pretty good. But wait until the two new cows he'd bought from Kressel freshened, and wait until he got some more cows, eight cows in all.

Emery followed the straggling column of cows among

the scrub apple trees down the little valley to the barn. His father and David were clicking the last stanchion bars shut when he got there.

After starting the milking machines, Emery and his father met in the alleyway and both grinned. It was clear they were both thinking: this is the big day; we're not under the thumb of the A.D. any more. But neither of them spoke the words.

David brought a pail and stool so that he could start to strip the cows. "Why can't they make a machine that'll milk a cow so she doesn't need to be stripped," he said, grumbling. "There isn't anything about dairying that I like—nothing."

Neither Emery nor his father said anything to him; they just continued to grin, accustomed to David's grousing.

When they went into the house for breakfast, Mrs. Crane was making doughnuts to be served with coffee at the Co-op station to celebrate the opening. Emery hurried through his meal and hauled their cans of milk down, pulling up behind the Spivacs' pickup in the line. Mary was unloading and he went to help her.

"Think they'll reject your milk, Mary?" he said.

She leaned back against the truck cab and laughed. Her hair was tucked up under a striped machinist's cap, the visor pulled low over her sparkling eyes. "It's hard to believe," she said. "Our own station; it's hard to believe."

The crowd increased rapidly. A dozen or more cars stood along the street and several trucks were parked at the edge of the cinder yard. Mrs. Lane and several other women were already serving coffee and doughnuts on improvised tables. By the time Emery had picked up his empties, his folks had arrived, and Bets and Mrs. Crane were helping.

He joined Mary. "Where are your folks? Are they coming later?"

"They can't come. They'll have to miss this. The bean pickers came this morning."

That reminded Emery of his own beans. They must be about ready for picking, too.

Jim Lane joined the crowd at the refreshment tables and Emery heard someone yell to him: "Hey, Jim, this time we've got the A.D. licked."

"They're never licked," Lane replied soberly. "Don't forget that. We'll have to go on fighting, but we've got something to fight with this time."

A cheer diverted the attention of the crowd, and Emery looked around to see Homer Carsen and his spring-wagon coming into the yard. The old dairyman pulled Sparks to a stop in the line, waiting to unload, and announced to the crowd: "I had the gol darndest time gettin' this old plug of mine to come here. He was all for goin' right on over to the A.D. like always. Stubborn old cuss. But I guess he's ree-conciled now—now he sees this is a milk station too."

Lane crossed the yard and patted the horse's head and gave him a lump of sugar. Old Sparks stood quietly, waiting his turn at the unloading conveyor.

Down at the beginning of the line Emery saw Nick Shostikov's truck and saw that Nick was talking to his father. He had thought that Nick was pulling out of the

Co-op, but when the two men separated, both were smiling, and Emery knew that Shostikov had decided to stick.

His glance shifted on to the street just as Del Bunce drove past in his new convertible.

Mary turned her back on the road, saying: "Let's go through our station, Em."

"Okay," he agreed, "let's make the tour."

As they passed the office, Emery saw David sitting at Sam Rudnek's desk, squinting into the eyepiece of a big microscope. He pulled open the door to the main room of the station and they were greeted by a din. Empty cans clattered, full cans thumped; motors hummed, driving the sterilizer, pumps, and cooler.

Sam Rudnek looked harassed. He was taking butterfat samples and smears for a bacteria count from each can of milk as it came through the swinging door.

Emery and Mary watched him work. They knew that Rudnek wanted to make a first test for the record on each patron's milk. After this first day's test, he would take smears only once a month except in unusual cases.

After Rudnek got his samples, one of the helpers dumped the cans into the weigher and recorded the number of pounds on a tag bearing the patron's number. Then the milk was piped into the cooler to be reduced quickly to a low temperature and pumped into the waiting tank truck. The empty cans then went clattering through the sterilizer where hissing steam jets washed them and the machine automatically sent them out on the conveyor to be picked up again by their owner.

When Emery and Mary came out past the office again,

David looked up, and seeing them, yelled: "Hey, Em, Mary, come here. This is fun!"

They joined him.

"Take a look in this microscope," David urged. "This is the reference slide Mr. Rudnek uses for checking."

Mary fixed one eye on the eyepiece.

"See that blue line," the boy said excitedly. "That's a mastitis strep. Isn't it a honey?"

A jointed blue line seemed to squirm among pink dots when Emery looked. Then David made an adjustment and let them look again. This time he showed them improperly cooled milk. By changing the slide, he showed them the various types of bacteria which could be found in bad milk.

Sam Rudnek came to the office door, his hair bristling around the edge of his white cap. "How about helping me, Dave?"

"Doing what?" asked the boy eagerly.

"Taking smears for the bacteria count."

"Just show me how." David started toward the door.

"Wait a minute," said Sam Rudnek. "Get into these overalls and jacket." He took a white outfit from the closet and tossed them to the boy.

The outfit was much too large for him and Emery and Mary laughed as David followed Sam up to the receiving platform, his face grimly serious. They went out to watch him take the cubic centimeter of milk from a patron's cans, smear it on a glass slide, jot down the patron's number on the slide, and put it aside to dry.

"Looks as if the kid has finally found something about dairying that he likes," Emery remarked to Mary.

By nine o'clock all the milk was in and some of the crowd had already gone home, but others still stood around the tables eating and talking. Above them the American flag snapped in the breeze and beneath it the pennant of the Co-op licked and curled.

Emery overheard Nels Peterson say to Jim Lane: "Wonder what happened over at the A.D. this morning—must have been kind of quiet around there."

"They've still got the big producers and the little fellows from east of Sheltonville," Jim pointed out.

"We'll show 'em though," Nels boasted.

"As long as we stick together they can't beat us," Mr. Lane replied. "But they'll try to break us up; they're going to be trying that every day now."

David came out of the station, still wearing his too-big uniform, but with a swagger. "Dad, can I stay? I want to help Mr. Rudnek make up the bacteria count record. I'll walk home." He looked from his father to Emery. "Please."

Mr. Crane nodded and the boy bounded back into the station, clothes flopping grotesquely.

"Jeepers!" Mary exclaimed. "I've been forgetting all about the bean picking. I'll have to go home."

Emery walked with her to the pickup truck. As she drove away, a big car pulled into the yard. It was Mr. Muller. He beckoned to Emery.

"The pickers will be over at your place in the morning," he said. "I'll have baskets dropped off for you this afternoon."

"All right, sir." Emery realized that Muller was ignoring the station completely, but otherwise he seemed friendly. "How're the beans turning out this year, sir?"

"Fine crop," Muller replied. "See you tomorrow." He swung his car back out to the street again.

Emery sauntered over to his truck. He guessed that Muller was burned up about the Co-op, but he was a big enough man not to let it make any difference in their business relations. As Emery drove away from the station, he glanced back at the sign, ATLAS DAIRIES CO-OP, INC. That was mighty nice, he told himself, and with a broad, happy grin on his face he sent the truck roaring up the road toward home.

Chapter Eleven

YELLOW GOLD

One of Muller's truckers brought the bean baskets and Emery helped him unload them by a scrub elm which grew near the drive that ran past the bean field. Before leaving, the truck driver squinted critically at the field.

"The pickers will like those beans," he said. "No weeds." Then he added: "Muller's got more beans share-cropped than he can handle unless he plans to give each patch just one picking."

The driver's concluding remark struck Emery—"one picking." What did he mean by that? A field was good for three pickings. But the trucker didn't give him a chance to ask.

At dinner Bets remarked that she was going out with Miss Prentis to inspect the migrant workers' living quarters in the county that afternoon. Emery started to ask which ones, but just then David arrived home from the milk station.

"Gee, I had fun," he cried, excitedly. "Dad, how much does a microscope like the one down there cost?"

"Two hundred and fifty dollars," replied Mr. Crane.

"That much? Aw gee!" The boy ate for a moment; then he said: "I'm going to help Sam with his records of the bacteria count. He says I can. Can't I do that, Dad?"

"I guess so," replied his father.

"I'm going to be a biologist or a chemist when I go to Cornell," David said. "I want to work a microscope."

His brother's discovery of a career pleased Emery, and he forgot about Bets' plans for the afternoon. That evening, riding home on a load of hay, he looked down at his bean field. In three pickings, he thought, he should get close to a thousand bushels, and if he averaged a dollar a bushel for his share, he'd clear a thousand dollars. But the recollection of the remark about "one picking" made him stop his dreaming.

At milking time, when he dumped the first full milker into a can, he saw Miss Prentis' car driving out of the yard, after bringing Bets home. When he came up to the house for supper, he noticed that his sister had been crying.

"What's the matter, Sis?" he asked.

She didn't answer, but at table she burst out: "You should see those shacks. Six and eight people living in a room no bigger than this dining room. They're no more than chicken coops. And there's no place for them to 'go' when they have to go except the cornfields . . ."

"Bets!" cried her mother. "You shouldn't talk like that while we're eating."

"Well, it's horrible," cried the girl indignantly. "There was a sick old Negro woman in a filthy bed, and another woman with a sick baby. No medicine, no care. We went to see Mr. Muller and he said he wasn't going to do anything about it. He said: 'those niggers like to live like that.' He said it was none of our business what kind of places he provided for them. Miss Prentis said she was going to report him to the Board of Health. He called us names. He called Miss Prentis a nosey old . . ." She looked frantically at her mother, then got up and fled to her room.

The rest of the family went on eating in silence.

Emery felt cold suddenly. Bets shouldn't have gone with Miss Prentis. Now she'd had a run-in with Muller. He remembered the driver's remark about one picking. And he owed Muller five hundred dollars—his Dad had signed that note too. He felt ashamed of himself for putting personal problems ahead of the welfare of those pickers, and that made him feel angry: Bets had no business getting mixed up in this.

In the morning, just as they were finishing the milking, Emery heard the pickers arrive. Their fluid talk and laughter echoed up to the barn. He saw about two dozen

Negroes, ranging from youngsters to old folks, starting into the field. The women and girls wore bright colored dresses. Beneath their broad-brimmed straw hats black faces gleamed in the slanting morning sunlight as if they had been freshly polished and waxed.

When Emery started with the milk to the Co-op station, he stopped for a moment to watch them working. A tall colored man brought a full basket up and set it beside the dozen full bushels already at the end of the field.

"You-all own this field?" he asked Emery.

"That's right."

"You-all mind if we get water to drink at yo' place?"

"Not at all. Help yourself."

"Thank yuh, suh." Bright teeth gleamed.

At the Co-op station, Emery saw the Spivac truck and looked for Mary. But Jack Spivac had brought their milk this morning and Emery asked him how his beans had turned out.

"Nothing to complain about, Em." A frown grew on Mr. Spivac's gray, wrinkled face. "But Muller said they'd hardly more than pay my share of seed and fertilizer and all that after he deducts the cost of picking and handling. It won't be until the next picking that I'll begin to get anything."

"Should be two more good pickings," Emery remarked.

"Should be." Mr. Spivac's eyes shifted to the Co-op station. "Now we have our own station, maybe us little dairymen can get out of the corner the big fellows got us into."

"Looks like we've got a chance," Emery replied.

"A fellow doesn't know which way to turn sometimes," Mr. Spivac said, grumbling. "They get you in a corner and squeeze."

Emery realized that Mr. Spivac was talking about his own difficult situation.

"I hear," the dairyman continued, "that Biggart's only picking the beans once for the farmers he's got signed up. He gave them just a word-of-mouth agreement."

"How can he make out himself doing that?" asked Emery quickly, a scared feeling gripping him.

"He charges twenty-five cents a bushel for picking and the farmer pays half, but he pays the pickers twenty cents. He charges half the hauling, but he hauls in his own trucks. Oh, Biggart does all right." Spivac chuckled dryly.

"Hope Muller doesn't try that with us," said Emery, worried.

"Can't." Spivac nodded his head with satisfaction. "We have written agreements. It says he has to pick 'em."

"Yes, that's right." Emery felt better.

As he started home through Atlas, Emery noticed how the village had come alive since the Co-op station opened up. The store had been repainted and groceries were displayed in the windows. A heap of lemons attracted his attention. He pulled the truck to the curb, entered the store, and bought two dozen.

At home he took an empty milk can up to the house, and Bets helped him make lemonade for the pickers. When he set the can and a supply of paper cups at the edge of the bean field two colored women were just bringing up full baskets.

"Here's some lemonade for you," he said.

"Lemonade! Why I declare," cried one of the women. "Thank you, white boy. We sho appreciate that."

The other woman, younger and cornstalk tall, yoo-hooed to the field. "Lemonade! Come on, you-all."

It took a moment for the other workers to realize what she'd said; then they swarmed toward the can.

"Mighty thoughtful of you," said one of the men to Emery as the others chattered, laughed, and gulped down the ice cold drink.

Emery grinned, feeling embarrassed.

A tall Negro youth remarked with a friendly smile: "Nice field of beans. Good picking." His voice was rich, but completely lacking the accent of the others.

"Next picking should be even better, I hope," Emery replied. There was an abrupt silence among the pickers.

Then one of the men said: "Nev' can tell; might not be a good nex' time."

"Jackson, you-all shut yo' mouth," said a woman sharply.

The young Negro spoke up. "Muller said to pick them close." He snatched up a bean just barely turning yellow from one of the baskets. "Like this. That means a smaller next picking—maybe not worth another picking at all."

"Oh he has to pick them again." Emery's voice sounded confident. "The agreement says so."

"The agreement . . ." The young Negro broke off abruptly.

On the way up to the house Emery looked back to see the pickers still talking beneath the scrub elm. He saw arms waving as if an argument was taking place;

then suddenly they were motionless. He saw the young Negro talking to them; then they spread out over the bean field and resumed picking.

That evening the beans, like baskets of yellow gold, were loaded on trucks to go to the New York City market, and Emery went down to the field to find out the total number of bushels. The pickers waited to be hauled to their shacks. As Emery approached, he saw Muller's car parked on the road and he heard Muller storming: "I told you niggers to pick close. You could have got another fifty . . ." He broke off.

A trucker had warned him of Emery's approach.

"Get rolling," he ordered the drivers. "Evening, Em."

"How'd the field make out, Mr. Muller?"

"Three hundred and eight bushels."

"That's pretty good, isn't it, sir?"

"We'll about break even on our expenses." Muller watched the full trucks start up. "We won't make much until next picking."

Emery felt relieved. Muller had said "next picking." Mr. Muller wasn't such a bad guy; and gee, after Bets and Miss Prentis had gotten into an argument with him over the living conditions of those Negroes just the other day, he might have been pretty nasty. Of course, there was the agreement—a written agreement . . .

Chapter Twelve

WRITTEN AGREEMENT

It was milking time when Emery came up from the bean field, so he went to the dairy. He found David in the workshop at the end of the barn patiently cutting pieces of broken window glass into small oblong sections.

"What're you doing?" Emery demanded.

His brother looked up eagerly. "I'm making slides. I'm going to take milk smears from each of our cows and test 'em for mastitis."

"Our cows haven't got mastitis," said Emery indignantly.

"Mr. Rudnek says there's a little in every herd."

Mr. Crane joined them and Emery reported the results of the bean picking, but he didn't say anything about the tongue-lashing he'd overheard Muller giving the pickers.

The following morning when Emery hauled the milk to the Co-op, David rode along, taking with him the slides he had finished. While Emery unloaded, the boy disappeared into the station office to check the smears under the microscope.

Mary Spivac had brought the milk from her father's dairy this morning, and Emery went to talk with her.

"How'd your beans turn out?" she wanted to know.

"Okay. But the next picking should be the best." Then he asked: "Has your dad heard how his beans sold?"

"Not yet." She hesitated a moment. "The pickers picked ours awfully close this first time."

"They didn't mine for some reason."

Emery saw his empty cans coming down the line and went to load them. As he finished, David joined him, carrying his slides. "No mastitis in that bunch," he announced.

"I told you there wouldn't be any," Emery said.

"I only tested eight." Then David looked up eagerly. "Mr. Rudnek says that all the Co-op herds should be tested the way I'm testing ours. Might avoid a lot of trouble sometime."

Emery didn't reply.

During the next few days the Cranes were busy putting up their second crop of alfalfa, and David didn't have time to make more tests. Then it rained and the haymaking had to stop, so David made six more slides. His report was the same as for the others—all clear.

It was still drizzling and the brothers drove over to Sheltonville where Emery had to do some shopping for his mother. In the grocery store he saw the young Negro who had talked to him the day of the bean-picking at his patch. The clerk, a sallow-faced, bald man, ignored the colored youth and waited on a woman first, then on two children.

"I'd like a pound of coffee," said the young Negro distinctly. "I've been waiting here a long time."

"You niggers can keep right on waiting," the clerk growled and moved along the counter toward Emery.

"I've a right to be waited on the same as anyone else," said the colored boy.

The air seemed to choke up in Emery's throat.

"So you want to start somethin', nigger?" retorted the clerk. "Open your trap again and I'll call a cop."

Emery choked out: "Go ahead and call a cop. Go on, and I'll go to court and say you refused to wait on this guy. We've laws against discrimination in this state!"

The clerk turned pale and filled the Negro's order. When he waited on Emery, he said placatingly: "They shouldn't bring those niggers up here. They're just a bunch of animals."

"We're all animals," snapped Emery. "Only some of us have manners!"

The clerk shut up, finished filling the order, and Emery stalked angrily out of the store. The colored youth was standing in the drizzling rain on the edge of the side-walk.

"Thanks a lot," he said, looking squarely into Emery's face. "Not many folks stand up for us around here."

"They can't treat you like that," Emery said angrily. Then he asked: "What's your name? Mine's Crane— Emery Crane."

"Walter Longstreth's mine." Then the young Negro continued haltingly: "Uh—don't know if I ought to tell you, but I think maybe I should. When we picked your beans, Muller ordered us to pick them clean; that usually means he doesn't intend to pick them again."

"He has to," said Emery. "The agreement says so."

"There are always ways of breaking agreements," Longstreth went on evenly, "when the big shots make them." His teeth flashed in a smile. "Thought I'd better warn you."

"Thanks. I'll be on the lookout for tricks."

All the way home, Emery worried about Walter Longstreth's warning. But I've a written agreement, he insisted over and over to himself.

That afternoon it stopped raining and Emery went to look at his beans. They hung in great handfuls on the bushes, just beginning to turn golden. The day after tomorrow they should be picked, he thought. The day after tomorrow for me; then tomorrow Muller should pick the Spivacs' beans.

In the morning he went to talk to Mary the moment she drove her father's pickup into the Co-op station yard.

"The pickers hadn't come by the time I left," she told him, her lips trembling a little. "And Muller didn't send any baskets last night either."

"Maybe they'll show up." Emery realized that his efforts to reassure were weak and he went home worrying again.

That afternoon, Muller sent no baskets for his field.

"The pickers are up at Bunce's," Mr. Crane told him. "Your beans can stand another day if they have to."

At the Co-op in the morning Emery watched anxiously for the Spivac pickup to arrive. It was apparently late, and he concluded hopefully that maybe the pickers had arrived at the Spivacs' after all. He waited for the return of his empties, watching the conveyor line. Suddenly he saw cans "31" on the line—they were Spivacs' cans. George Kressel began loading them on his truck, and Emery hurried over to ask about the Spivacs.

"They're picking beans." Kressel slammed the last can onto his truck. "Muller ran out on the second picking and they're trying to save what they can. Their problem is a market. Maybe they can get rid of a few in Syracuse or Utica."

Emery decided that he'd better find out what Muller intended to do about his beans. The big dairyman was up at Del Bunce's bean field. "Morning, Em," he greeted, "What're you in such a lather about?" He grinned slyly.

"Are you going to pick my beans, Mr. Muller?"

"Can't make it." Muller looked regretful about it.

"But our agreement says you—you have to pick them."

"I know it says I have to pick them or the patch is yours." Muller shrugged. "Guess I'll have to let you take the patch—a good patch, too. The sale of the first picking just squared things between us. The rest are all yours."

Emery swallowed hard. What good were those beans to him? He couldn't pick them or sell them. "But how'll I pay back the money you've loaned me unless you pick them?"

"Your father's signature's on the note; maybe he'll help you out," Muller replied.

The sick feeling in Emery's stomach grew.

Del Bunce joined them, looked at Emery, and guffawed. "He looks sick before he even starts eating all those beans."

"Get those pickers straightened out?" asked Muller.

"Sure," Bunce replied.

"Let's get rolling, then," Muller continued. "We've got to get over to my south field."

They walked over to Bunce's convertible and drove off.

Emery realized now that Muller had planned all this from early spring: get the small dairymen to agree to raise beans for him, get them in debt to him, then pull out, leaving them to wiggle and squirm. How many small dairymen had he tied up this way? Emery's jaws felt stiff with sudden terror. These deals had been made before the Co-op was started. A lot of the small dairymen sharecropping beans were Co-op members. Would Muller use this debt hold over them now to help the A.D. break the Co-op?

A picker yelled at him, and he saw Walter Longstreth coming across the field.

"Muller not picking for you?" Walter asked.

"That's right." Emery's lips were dry.

"You'll have to get them picked by tonight and to the city tomorrow morning or you'll miss the weekend market," Walter pointed out.

Emery licked frantically at his dry lips. He hadn't thought of that angle. "Guess I'm sunk," he admitted.

"If I can think of something," Walter offered. "Maybe if I talk to the others." Then he added: "Sorry about it," and turned back to the field.

Emery stopped at the Co-op to pick up David who had stayed to check more slides. The moment his brother got into the truck, he said, "One of your cows has mastitis."

For a moment, Emery didn't grasp what David meant. Then he retorted angrily: "You're crazy. My cows are all right."

"They're not either," cried his brother. "One of those two you milk first has mastitis. It shows up on the slides. Tonight, milk them separately so that I can take smears from each; then I'll be able to tell which one it is."

"You're crazy," Emery yelled. "Don't go talking nonsense. My cows haven't got mastitis, I tell you!"

David was scared into silence by his brother's anger.

All the way home Emery's mind seethed: what was he going to do? He couldn't meet the note to Muller on August fifteenth. His Dad would have to help him and that would mean they couldn't meet debts coming due the first of September. He had forgotten the bigger threat to the Co-op; the threat to the Cranes was big enough right now. Maybe he'd have to sell his cows. And there was the beautiful field of beans which would go to waste.

He brought the truck to a screeching stop at the milkhouse and yelled at David: "Unload those empties. I've got to find Dad."

He leaped out of the cab and ran toward the back field where his father was cutting more hay.

Chapter Thirteen

"JOSHUA FIT THE BATTLE"

Emery shouted at his father: "Muller's not going to pick the beans. What're we going to do?"

Mr. Crane let the tractor idle. "I don't know what we can do." Then he cut the ignition switch and they walked up to the house.

"Everybody's over at the Spivacs' picking beans," Bets informed them. "That's where we ought to be."

"Yes," replied her father. "Maybe we can get the folks helping them today to help us tomorrow."

"Let's go then," said Emery. Then he remembered

what Walter had said about the weekend market and realized that tomorrow would be too late.

The Cranes found the Spivac yard full of automobiles and a crowd in the bean field. Jack Spivac came to meet them.

"I was going to call you folks," he said, "but I figured you had your own beans to worry about."

"We can't handle them alone," replied Mr. Crane. "We came to help you; maybe you can give us a hand tomorrow."

"Sure." Mr. Spivac's gray, wrinkled face hardened. "I'd give a lot if we could beat Muller on this deal."

Emery grabbed a basket and joined the pickers. For a long time he worked steadily, not looking up, trying not to think.

He knew that Mary was somewhere in the field, but he didn't want to see her. He didn't feel like talking to anyone. A tightness, almost a lump, in his throat made him miserable. He told himself that he was glad they were saving the Spivacs' crop, but that wouldn't help him any. In two more weeks he'd have to pay Muller and there would be no money to pay with.

After filling his second basket, he realized that he was alone in the field. The pickers were gathering at the upper end to eat lunch. When he tried to straighten, he thought his spine would crack. This bean picking was no picnic. How did those colored folks stand it day after day?

Emery joined the crowd sitting in the shade of a big sugar maple eating sandwiches and drinking iced coffee. They joked and kidded and laughed. Then someone mentioned Muller and his name dampened them down at once.

"I wonder what he figures by not picking his share-cropped beans," remarked George Kressel.

"I can tell you what he figures," spoke up Nels Peterson angrily. "I owe him some money—gotta pay this coming Tuesday. He told me he couldn't pick my beans the way he agreed but he'd extend my note for two months provided—provided I sell my stock in the Co-op and come back to the A.D."

So that was it. Emery wondered if any other Co-op members had been similarly approached. The thought scared him: how many might accept that way out of a jam? Maybe when the fifteenth of August came, Muller would offer to extend his note if he'd pull out of the Co-op.

"But I've outfoxed him," Peterson continued. "My beans'll be ready to pick Monday. I've contracted the crop to a canning factory up near Morris Springs, so if you folks'll help me the way you're helping Jack, I'll have Muller beat."

The neighbors agreed without hesitation to help Nels. And Peterson's custom-canning of his beans gave Emery an idea—maybe he could contract his crop to a canning factory. His appetite improved and he took another sandwich. He glanced eagerly around, hoping to see Mary now, but she was up at the house helping her mother.

He did see his father, Jim Lane, and Jack Spivac talking. Scrambling to his feet, he approached them. "Dad, how about hunting up a canning factory for my beans?"

Mr. Crane shook his head, while Jim Lane explained: "All the canneries around here are contracted full, Em.

Muller's got a lot of them tied up—Muller, Biggart, and Howells, and the little farmers the rest of 'em."

"I tried to get in," Spivac said. "Couldn't for ten days. I'm just lucky to make the weekend market in Syracuse."

That reminded Emery that unless his beans were picked today and marketed tomorrow, they'd miss the weekend buyers. He knew that his father realized this now.

"How about canneries down Binghamton way," said Mr. Crane.

"You might find one not tied up," Jim Lane said.

"Better get in your car and go down there," advised Spivac. "We can get my beans picked without you, Lou."

Emery watched his father go to their car and drive off. The neighbors were struggling back to the field and he resumed picking. As he moved along a row, he was aware that someone was coming toward him, picking the next row.

"Emery, I'm sorry about your beans being left too."

His head jerked up. Mary crouched by a half-filled basket, her large blue eyes full of sympathy as she looked at him. A red bandanna held back her dark hair and her tanned face was moist with perspiration.

"Guess I'm in for a beating." He tried to toss the reply off nonchalantly.

"Dad's not going to get enough from our beans to pay Muller what we owe him," she said. "Not by half."

"Oh." Emery look at her sharply, wondering suddenly if her father would be forced to pull out of the Co-op.

"I don't know what we're going to do," she said.

"Hope you get a break." He felt helpless.

They continued picking in silence, each going in the opposite direction.

Toward evening, David came to see him. "It's time to milk," he said. "I'll go home and do it and you can stay here—you and Mom and Bets."

Emery glanced at the sun, then into his brother's anxious face. "Thought you didn't like milking."

"Better than bean picking. Besides, I want . . ." David stopped, then added: "Please, Em, let me take care of the milking; I'm sick of picking beans."

"Okay," Emery agreed. His brother hurried away and Emery wondered about this sudden enthusiasm for milking. Then he remembered David's saying this morning that one of his two cows, Star or Tassel, had mastitis. He shrugged. Oh well, let him milk them separately and make the tests; it wouldn't hurt anything. He returned to picking beans.

The job was finished a little after six o'clock and Jim Lane took the Cranes home. On the way Emery remarked: "We ought to have a Co-op for beans just as we have one for milk."

Jim Lane gave him a sidewise, thoughtful glance. "You've got something there, Em." Then he watched his driving.

David was just turning the cows out of the barn when they arrived home. As the family finished a hasty supper, Mr. Crane drove into the yard and came up to the house. They knew by his walk that he'd found no market for the beans.

"Guess I'm licked," Emery said dejectedly.

Bets turned eagerly away from looking out the window. "Here comes Chuck," she announced.

His car swung to a quick stop and he came striding up to the house, a big grin on his face.

"You gave Dad an idea on the way home, Em," Chuck said excitedly. "He called up Mr. Sandler at the Consumers' Co-op that takes the milk from our station. He had a hard time finding his home telephone number. But Mr. Sandler told Dad that if you could get the beans down there by seven o'clock in the morning, he could find a market for you."

The Cranes brightened up: A market! But at 7 A.M.!

"If the beans were picked," said Mr. Crane.

That fact pounded at Emery's brain: if only those beans were picked.

"We'll come over and help pick them," Chuck volunteered. "Maybe some of the other folks'll come."

"But everybody's tired out," lamented Mrs. Crane.

"I can pick some more," said Bets, smiling at Chuck.

"But tonight—how can we pick them tonight?"

"There's a full moon." Bets pointed out of the window at the golden disk in the eastern sky.

"We might save part of the crop," Emery said.

Mr. Crane stepped to the telephone and called the Spivacs. He explained the situation to Mr. Spivac. Emery waited nervously through a long pause in the conversation, feeling his hands growing clammy.

"Thanks, Jack," his father said into the telephone. "Bring all the baskets you can, and tell the others, will you?"

He turned back into the room. "They're coming, and Mrs. Spivac is going to call everyone she can reach and get as many others as she can to help."

Chuck Lane drove home to bring back his folks, and the Cranes, hunting up all the available baskets they could find, set out at once for the bean patch. Emery scanned the sky hopefully. It was clear and the full moon already stood well above the horizon.

In a short time the neighbors began to arrive. They shouted greetings, talked, and kidded as if this were a picnic. But faces showed lines of fatigue in the dusk. Someone stooping to pick would groan, but that brought laughter—it seemed better than liniment for their aching muscles.

Mary Spivac picked the row next to Emery.

"Gee, I'm glad you found a market, Em."

"Guess we'll save part of the crop," he said.

There were twenty-five or thirty pickers at work, but they would never cover the patch by midnight, he knew, and the beans had to be loaded to leave by twelve o'clock if they were to get to the city by seven in the morning.

"If there were just more help," Mary remarked.

The moon gathered luminosity, lighting the field. When they tipped up the bean vines, the golden beans seemed to throw off light of their own.

"Sounds like someone singing." Mary tilted her head, listening.

"Guess somebody must have left his car radio going," Emery suggested. "Not a bad idea."

Then both of them straightened up. The music came from the road and they could hear the words distinctly.

"Joshua fit the battle of Jericho, Jericho, Jericho,
Joshua fit the battle of Jericho,
And the walls came tumblin' down."

Down the road came a straggling line of figures. Emery and Mary and the neighbors all stared in amazement.

Mary whispered: "Those are the colored pickers."

"What 're they doing out here?" somebody asked from a few rows over.

Emery didn't say anything; he couldn't find words. Then he started at a run across the field, leaping over the bean rows, racing madly to meet the approaching column on the highway.

Chapter Fourteen

THE LONG RIDE

Emery halted when he reached the edge of the field, suddenly doubting that the Negroes had really come to help. It didn't seem to him that anything like that could happen. He saw Walter Longstreth leading the line.

"Need some help, Emery?" called Walter.

"Sure could use some," he replied thickly.

Walter joined him and both turned to look at the field in the moonlight while the newcomers paused to rest.

"After supper, I talked my friends into taking a walk over," Walter explained.

"Quite a walk—four miles. It—it was mighty swell of you." Emery still found talking difficult.

"I didn't know whether you'd found a market or not, but I figured we could take that chance."

One of the colored pickers spoke up: "If'n the Bossman finds out you-all figured us into this, Walter, you-all is goin' to get into trouble."

Young Longstreth laughed. "It was a nice walk in the moonlight wasn't it, Aunty Sara?"

"As tarred as I is, no walkin's nice."

Among the resting pickers someone started humming *Swing Low, Sweet Chariot*. The song grew, then tapered off and died.

A man said: "Walt, let's get to pickin'."

Emery started them into the field, asking Walter to keep track of the baskets picked so that he could pay them.

One of the pickers remarked: "Ain't bad this pickin' in the moonlight—ain't bad 'tall."

"Hope Bossman Muller don't get the idea though."

Someone started singing *Swing Low, Sweet Chariot* again and the song, with more voices added, moaned over the bean field.

Emery returned to his basket. Mary had picked his row along with hers so that they could go on picking together. It was nine o'clock, three hours before the loaded beans had to start to market.

"How'd those colored folks happen to come?" asked Mary.

"It was Walter's idea." Then Emery told her how he had gotten acquainted with Longstreth.

"I think they're wonderful," Mary murmured.

Over the field the sound of singing grew. Sometimes a voice shot up shrilly, a weird knife-sharp complaint. The song rose and fell, flattened, and swelled. The singers began swinging the melody, wildly, furiously; then it grew calm again, tapering to softness. It came back rich and strong.

Nick Shostikov was the first of the neighbors to join the singing. His baritone suddenly rolled forth from that side of the field. Others joined in now, singing the words if they knew them, or just humming the tune if they didn't.

And the number of full baskets grew at the end of the field. At eleven o'clock Emery stopped picking to help his father load their truck. It didn't take them long to realize that they needed another truck.

"I'll get mine," Jim Lane said and went home for it.

By a quarter of twelve the last of the beans were picked and the pickers rested along the drive; the singing ended too. But the neighbors and the migrant pickers mingled, talking, occasionally joking as only the dog-tired can joke. Then Bets came down and invited them to supper up on the lawn.

Walter helped Emery and Mr. Crane and Jim Lane lash down the baskets of beans on the trucks.

When the last rope was hitched, Emery turned to Walter. "I've asked George Kressel to take you folks home," he said. "I don't know how to thank you for what you've done. Tomorrow I'll come over and pay for the picking."

"Better not come over to Muller's." Walter's face was

sober in the moonlight. "Would it be all right if I came over here tomorrow night?"

"Sure." All the fatigue of the day caught up with Emery at once and he slouched against the truck. "I certainly appreciate what you've done, Walt." His voice choked out on him.

"It's been fun." Walter smiled. "And—and maybe a little educational for all of us."

"I guess we'd better get rolling," said Mr. Crane.

Emery and his father climbed into their truck and Jim Lane into his and they headed for New York City.

"You'd better take a snooze, Em," said Mr. Crane. "You can take the wheel from Jim or me later. I don't feel sleepy now, but I'm going to before morning."

Emery slumped back into the corner of the cab and in spite of the jolting was soon sound asleep. The little convoy rolled east on Route 20, then turned off on Route 145 toward the Hudson River. Emery slept until they stopped at the toll booth on the Rip Van Winkle Bridge.

"How're you doing, Dad?" he asked, aroused now.

"Okay. Have a good nap?"

Emery yawned. "Gee, my neck feels like a pretzel."

"We'd better pull up when we get across the bridge," said Mr. Crane, "and see how Jim's making out."

When they stopped, Lane joined them, choking a yawn. "Sleep's just about got me licked," he admitted, "and I don't want to spill Em's beans over the landscape."

"I'm still all right," said Mr. Crane. "I'll take your truck and Emery can drive ours so you can nap."

They rolled along Route 9G toward the Albany Post

Road. The sky was light in the east by the time they passed through Poughkeepsie. Below Fishkill they stopped at a diner for breakfast. Mr. Crane was getting sleepy by this time, but Lane was ready to take the wheel again. He took the lead now because he knew where the beans had to be delivered and they rolled on. By six o'clock they were entering the Bronx.

Emery wondered if they'd make it on time. He wished Jim would crowd his truck more as they rolled along, keeping pace with the changing traffic signals.

"I hope Jim's sure of where he's going," Emery worried aloud. "If we get lost, I'm sunk."

On and on down the east side of Manhattan they drove. Emery didn't know where they were exactly; once he glimpsed the Empire State Building, but he was too tired to do much looking around.

Suddenly Jim's truck swung east and climbed up over a bridge above the East River. More turns and twists followed. Emery felt dazed; he just followed the load of beans in front. It pulled over to a long platform and slowed to a stop.

What was Jim stopping for, Emery wondered for a moment; then he realized that they had arrived. He looked at his watch—ten minutes to seven. His father was still asleep.

A man came down the platform and talked with Jim Lane. Emery got out of the cab stiffly and joined them just as the man said: "Glad you fellows made it. Sandler warned me to expect you."

Other trucks roared and ground gears in the street. Along the platform loads of produce were being dumped or reloaded. The man on the platform pointed out a spot for them to unload; they backed their trucks into it and began setting off the baskets of beans—four hundred and fifteen of them.

"Good beans." The man snapped one between his fingers. "Too bad the market's no better than it is. Two dollars a bushel is the best we can pay you."

Emery tried to figure out what this price would net him for the beans, but he was too tired to add numbers. "Okay," he said, and followed the man into the office and waited for the cashier to make out the check. He mumbled his thanks, while his bleary eyes tried to read the numbers on the green slip of paper; then he slipped it into his pocket.

When he returned to the trucks, his father and Jim Lane were talking to a stocky, round-headed man.

"This is Mr. Sandler, Emery," Jim Lane said.

"Did you get your check?" asked Mr. Sandler.

"Yes, sir. Thanks for getting us a market."

"I'm mighty glad I was able to," replied Mr. Sandler. "We want you folks up there to make that new Co-op solid. The big producers up there are out to get you small dairymen, and if you didn't know it before, you know it now." Then, wishing them luck, and shaking hands with all three, he walked briskly out to his car which was parked in the street.

Jim Lane paused at the door of his truck and asked: "Want to stay and see the sights of New York City, Emery?"

"No thanks," he replied, "let's go home."

His father and Lane laughed, and the three climbed

into the trucks for the homeward trip. Traffic was thicker now. It took longer to get out of the city and rolling up the Hudson, but Emery slept through it all. They arrived back in Sheltonville just before the bank closed.

The bank teller examined the check Emery gave him suspiciously. "This any good?" he asked.

"Sure," Emery snapped. "I'm depositing it; put it through and you can see if it's any good."

The teller looked around for Mr. Haley, shrugged, then made the notation of deposit in Emery's bank book.

When he rejoined his father in the truck, Emery exploded angrily at the way the bank teller had treated him.

"Could be they don't like to see you get money," said Mr. Crane chuckling. "If you pay Muller, you'll be one Co-op member they won't have a club over."

Emery remembered the offer Muller had made to Nels Peterson. Some such offer was awaiting him if he couldn't pay. His spine tingled with a feeling of triumph: he could pay Muller, and promptly on August fifteenth he would pay him.

Chapter Fifteen

DEBT PAID

When Emery and Mr. Crane got out of the truck at the milkhouse, they saw David and Bets down in the barn and saw one of the cows standing in a stall. It was Emery's milker, Tassel. Her udder was encased in a canvas bag, held in place by cords tied up over her hips.

"She's the one with mastitis," David explained hurriedly. "I took the smear last night and I showed Sam the slide this morning. 'It's just starting,' he said. Treating her was Bets' idea." He gave his sister a quick, scared look. "We figured we could stop it before it got any worse. We did just what the book says to do . . ."

Emery interrupted angrily: "After this you let me take care of my own cows."

"If Sam says she showed mastitis," remarked their father casually, "then that treatment should start clearing it up. The sooner the treatment the better."

Emery didn't say any more, but he was still indignant because his cow had been accused of having mastitis.

As they started to leave the barn, Mr. Crane asked: "How was everything at the station this morning, Dave?"

"The milk tanker was late," the boy replied. "Sam had all the storage tanks full. He says we need another storage tank."

Mr. Crane shook his head soberly. "If that tanker is too late some time, we'll be in real trouble."

Emery didn't pay much attention to this conversation; his thoughts were on his own business. Gee, last night seemed months ago. Tonight Walter was coming over to collect the pay for the Negro pickers.

But it was after nine o'clock before Walter got there. "I had a hard time getting away," he explained. "We're being watched so that we can't help anybody else."

"How can Muller keep you from going out?" asked Bets.

"He can't really," Walter said, "but he might frame us for something. My friends are easily intimidated." After a pause he asked: "Was the Co-op tanker late this morning?"

Emery looked startled. "David said it was. Why?"

"I just happened to hear a couple of Muller's truckers talking while the beans were being loaded tonight," Walter said. "One of them had his arm in a cast but he was still driving a truck. Muller doesn't carry compensation on his truckers, you know; he makes them show up at the dairy barns at night and pretend to help with the milking. That lets him list them as farm help instead of truckers, and he doesn't have to carry compensation on farm help. So this fellow has to go on driving a truck or he doesn't get paid. Anyhow, I heard him say he wasn't going to lay for the Co-op tanker and try to delay it the way Muller had ordered them to do. He didn't want to get mixed up in any tricks like that with one arm, he said."

"How do they delay the tanker?" Emery asked, anxiously.

A shrug was Walter's answer, but Mr. Crane spoke up: "A bunch of those empty bean trucks loafing ahead of that big tanker could slow it up a lot."

"I suppose they could," Emery admitted. "I hadn't thought of that."

Walter stood up. "I'd better get back to the shacks," he said. "Aunty Sara's come down sick with something. We haven't been able to get a doctor to come out . . ." He broke off abruptly, then added: "I promised to bring her some aspirin."

"I'll call Miss Prentis, Walter," Bets offered. "I'll call her first thing in the morning and we'll come over."

"Those shacks are no place for you," Walter replied. "But we'll appreciate it if you'll tell Miss Prentis. It's her job."

"I'll come with her. I'm not afraid," Bets insisted.

Walter's teeth flashed as he smiled in the dusk.

Emery drove him back to Muller's farm, letting him

out near a corn field, so that he could slip back to the shacks unnoticed. On the way home Emery thought about the big producers' trick of delaying the Co-op tanker. Why can't they leave us alone, he complained bitterly to himself; we'd do fine if they'd leave us alone.

In the morning David went with him when he delivered the milk. He had taken a new smear from Tassel and wanted to check it under the microscope to see if she showed any improvement from the treatment he and Bets had given her.

After unloading the milk Emery joined David in the Co-op office.

"There's no trace this morning," David said gleefully. "We fixed her up." He adjusted a slide. "Here, give a look. This is the one that showed."

Emery squinted into the eyepiece.

"See that little chain of blue in the center?" When Emery grunted, David continued: "That's the mastitis strep—just starting. You see, Tassel *did* have it."

Emery didn't reply.

"Here's the slide I made this morning." David made the change quickly. "Now take a look."

This time Emery saw no blue dots.

"See, all clear. We caught her just in time."

"Yeah," Emery grudgingly admitted.

"If we'd let her go," David said, "she'd soon have been so bad your milk would have been rejected."

Loud voices in the yard attracted their attention. A long line of trucks waited at the receiving conveyor and the boys realized that the tanker was late again.

Sam Rudnek was explaining to the dairymen: "It's

the bean trucks. Yesterday, five of Biggart's empties got ahead of our tanker. The driver couldn't get past them."

"We need an extra storage tank," one farmer said.

Emery saw Jack Spivac in the crowd and was struck immediately by the haggard look on his face. As he was the only member of the Co-op board of directors present, several of the dairymen urged him to call a directors' meeting and do something about this problem right away.

"That's what I'm going to do," Spivac replied, and his voice shook as if he were angry.

Emery saw Mary in her father's truck and went to talk with her.

"Aren't you glad you got rid of your beans?" she asked the moment he approached.

"Sure am. But I don't think Muller is."

She laughed, then quickly sobered. "Dad didn't do so well with ours. He can't pay all he owes Mr. Muller, but Mr. Muller promised to carry us along for awhile."

"That's not so good." Emery looked away quickly.

"Dad said Mr. Muller seemed friendly. He didn't ask him to quit the Co-op." Mary's tone seemed to plead for Emery's understanding. "I guess it'll work out."

"I hope so, Mary."

That evening Bets came home from her visit with Miss Prentis to Aunty Sara in the migrant workers' shacks. The old woman was running a very high temperature, Bets reported, and Miss Prentis had had her taken to the hospital in Sheltonville. Then Miss Prentis talked Mr. Humbert into coming out to see the conditions at the shacks. When Mr. Muller found out, he was furious. But

Miss Prentis again reported the whole mess to the Board of Health and Mr. Humbert said he was going to start a clean-up campaign in the *News-Star*.

"I think Miss Prentis and Mr. Humbert kind of like each other," Bets finished, her face glowing.

Mr. Lane came over and announced that Jack Spivac had asked him to call a board meeting to do something about more storage at the station.

"When did the tanker get here today?" asked Mr. Crane.

"Ten-thirty," Lane said. "The bean trucks were waiting for it again. But our driver tried to duck them; then a trooper gave him a ticket and that held him up two hours."

"We'd better figure out something," Mr. Crane said.

"I've told the other board members we'd meet Saturday night," Lane told him.

On Saturday night, Emery waited up for his father to come home from the meeting. "What happened?" he asked as soon as Mr. Crane came into the living room.

"Considerable. We're going to buy an old tank trailer from the A.D. The tank's still all right—it'll store twenty-five hundred gallons. Spivac's arranging the deal."

Emery remembered Mary's telling him that Muller had extended her father's loan; now Mr. Spivac was helping the A.D. get rid of an old tanker. Did all this fit together?

His father continued: "Six more members have asked us to buy back their shares—seventeen hundred dollars worth. Charlie Bullock's buying seven shares. I don't know where he's getting seven hundred dollars in a lump. I promised to take two of the other shares." He sighed.

"I guess your mother won't get running water in the house this fall."

"Can't we re-sell them to new members, Dad?"

Mr. Crane shook his head. "The A.D. is bending over backwards to hold its present patrons and win ours back. We'd hoped to offset the A.D.'s better payments by declaring a dividend from profits, but buying this tank for storage will eat up all our profits. They're fighting us with everything they've got and that's plenty."

For a long time that night Emery lay awake worrying. If the Co-op failed, maybe he and his father would be blacklisted by the A.D. and that would end any possibility of his ever renting the old Armstrong place and starting dairying on his own. Anyhow, he told himself finally, he could pay Muller Monday. After that, he fell asleep.

Del Bunce was in Muller's office when Emery stopped.

"The Boss is over showing the Board of Health his nigger houses," Bunce said. "I can take care of any business you've got with him—I'm his office manager."

"Aren't you going to Cornell next month?" Emery asked.

"Who wants to go to Cornell? I've got a big chance right here working for Mr. Muller."

Emery grinned. He saw Mr. Muller, accompanied by two strangers and Miss Prentis and Mr. Humbert, approaching cars parked in front of the office. Muller's face was an angry red. From where Emery stood in the office he heard one of the strangers say: "That's orders. One family to a cabin and all the places must be fumigated and whitewashed. And separate quarters must be provided for the single help."

Muller nodded curtly. The others got into their cars and drove off and he came on toward his office, his manner changing the moment he saw Emery.

"What can I do for you, son?" he asked pleasantly.

"I came to pay my note," replied Emery.

"You're a businesslike young man." Muller took his check, glanced at it, scribbled "cancelled" across the face of the note and initialed it. As he handed it to Emery, he asked: "Still want to get started dairying on your own?"

"As soon as I can, sir."

"I admire the enterprise you showed in selling your beans," Muller praised. "Shows you can succeed. I'll start you dairying any time you're ready. How about it?"

Emery gulped. "Thanks, sir. Have to think about it."

He was aware that Del Bunce was glaring furiously as he walked out of the office. All the way home he pondered Muller's offer: gee, here was a chance to become a dairyman right away—if—if he could just trust Muller.

MORE TROUBLE

But Emery knew that any offer from Muller wasn't to be trusted; the bean deal had taught him that. Muller was a big dairyman and although he wasn't on the A.D. Committee, all the big dairymen and the A.D. were out to absorb the little dairymen and to break the Co-op.

One morning the following week when he stopped at the Co-op office to tell David he was ready to go home, Leo Reilly was inside arguing with Mr. Rudnek about his milk.

"But Leo, you can smell it yourself," Sam was saying.

"Maybe a little." Reilly's face was an angry red. "You're getting as fussy as the A.D."

David interrupted: "Sam, it's mastitis. I've just found it on this slide. There's mastitis somewhere in Leo's herd."

"That's not so," said Reilly indignantly.

Sam looked into the microscope. "Yes, that's mastitis. Take a look, Leo."

Reilly looked and shook his head. "Might be for all I know. Gadgets like that can fool me."

"You can't fool the microscope," said Sam. "The Co-op has to keep the milk clean. If a whole tank load gets bad, then everyone in the Co-op will suffer."

David continued to examine slides; suddenly he announced: "It's only one can, Sam. I took smears from each of Leo's cans and only one shows the mastitis strep."

Rudnek's face brightened. "We'll need to reject only that one can in that case."

"Well, that's not too bad." Reilly took a deep breath.

David spoke up eagerly: "You ought to let me make slides from each cow, Leo. Once you find out which one has it you can fix her up in a little while."

Emery spoke up: "The kid discovered that one of my cows had it, Leo. He caught her before she was bad enough to get my milk rejected."

"Come over tonight and do your stuff," said Reilly gruffly. Then he glared at Sam: "I own seven shares of Co-op stock and I can't afford to be pushed around."

"Nobody's pushing you around, Leo," Rudnek replied.

Reilly hustled his rejected can of milk out to his truck

and drove over to wait for the empties at the far conveyor. Emery returned to the yard and stopped to talk to Mary who had merely accompanied her father this morning. At the moment Mr. Spivac was talking to Dan Jessup.

The line of waiting trucks moved along and Spivac came to drive the pickup ahead, but before he got there, Mary whispered: "Something's the matter with Dad lately. I thought everything . . ." She didn't finish.

Her father climbed in beneath the wheel, with only a nod toward Emery. He started the motor; then he asked: "What's the matter with Leo this morning?"

Emery told him about the rejected can of milk.

Spivac's eyes narrowed thoughtfully; then without replying, he drove the pickup forward in the line.

David talked about his assignment excitedly on the way home. Every Co-op member should have a bacteria test made of his herd. That was a job he'd like to do.

He went over to Reilly's at milking time and didn't get home until after nine o'clock. Then he came breezing into the house. "We found two of Leo's cows had it," he said proudly. He had made the slides, then Leo and he had taken them to the station, and Sam had checked them under the microscope.

"How'd Leo take it?" inquired his father.

"All right," David replied. "How else could he?"

In the morning, Emery saw Reilly in the line-up, saw him send in his milk and pick up his empties. Apparently he had kept out the infected milk for none was rejected.

When Emery went over to talk with Mary while waiting, he noticed at once that her eyes were red as if she had been crying. "What's the matter, Mary?"

Her lips trembled. "You'd better go back to your truck, Em. Dad's in a terrible temper this morning. He had a quarrel with Muller yesterday."

He stared at her in surprise: what did she mean? Then he saw Spivac coming to the pickup and, with a nod, he turned away. The dairyman ignored him completely.

After picking up his empty cans, Emery drove over to Sheltonville for a load of cow feed. All the way he puzzled over Mary and her father's strange behavior: what had happened? In Sheltonville he saw Leo Reilly talking with Del Bunce and that gave him something more to puzzle over.

At least that part was cleared up that evening when Jim Lane called and told Mr. Crane that Reilly was pulling out of the Co-op. Mr. Crane had to go down to a director's meeting.

After supper Emery tried to read but couldn't keep his mind on the book so he offered to help Bets with the dishes. "You all set to start your nurse's training?" he asked.

"Just one more uniform to make," she told him eagerly, then rattled on with all the details of her preparations.

He encouraged her to talk and she told him about going with Miss Prentis to inspect Muller's place again. All the shacks had been whitewashed and a barn had been turned into a dormitory for the unmarried pickers with a dispensary in one of the stalls and a recreation room in the loft.

Emery wondered what had happened to Walter Longstreth; he hadn't seen him lately. Bets' talk kept his mind off Co-op problems, but when he returned to the living room the thought of Reilly dumping seven shares of stock started him worrying again. That would be a blow to the Co-op.

At bedtime he said: "Guess I'll wait up for Dad."

Then David buried his head deeper in a comic magazine and said: "Guess I'll wait up too."

It was almost eleven before Mr. Crane came in.

"The A.D.'s taking Reilly back," he announced. Then he turned to David. "Bad news for you, Dave. You're to stay away from the Co-op after this."

"Why?" The boy stared at him big-eyed.

"Spivac and Bullock said you were making trouble. Jim, Nels and I stuck up for you, but Spivac, Bullock, Hollis and Carsen voted you out." He didn't give David a chance to reply to this. "I don't know what's eating Jack. He says we can't baby patrons. If their milk's bad, Sam's to reject it. He's not to bother to test it. Jack insisted that Sam be officially directed to do this, and Bullock, Carsen, and Hollis supported him."

"How's Dave's helping Co-op members to clear up bad milk babying them?" Emery asked.

"That's what Jim and I argued, but they wouldn't listen to us."

"We can't go on losing members," Emery said.

"That we can't." Then Mr. Crane slowly shook his head. "The way Jack acts has got me stumped. He won't listen to anyone."

"Who's buying Reilly's stock?" asked Emery.

"I'm buying one share, Jim's buying two, and Bullock's buying the other four."

Emery's forehead wrinkled up. "That'll give Charlie Bullock fifteen shares, won't it?"

His father nodded.

"Where's he getting the money?"

"I don't know. I'll have to go to the bank myself."

That prospect made them silent for awhile.

David's face had grown longer and longer. "Dad, won't they even let me help Sam with the bacteria count?"

"No. Spivac says you're not to fool around the office any more."

"Fool around!" David snorted indignantly. "I hope all of old Spivac's cows get mastitis."

"Don't talk like that," ordered Emery angrily.

"Aw, you're just soft on Mary . . ."

"It's time we were all in bed," said their father.

"I'd like to fix old man Spivac," threatened David. "I'd . . ."

"That's enough now, Dave," repeated Mr. Crane sternly.

They heard of no more milk being rejected during the next few days; then one morning Emery noticed Nick Shostikov's truck parked out in front of the office and Nick came out making little sidewise shakes with his head.

"Three bad ones," he announced. "Three good—I don't figure." He just seemed puzzled, not mad.

"I'm sorry," Emery said, hoping to placate Nick. He helped the dairyman reload the three rejected cans on his truck. His hands felt cold at the touch of each can.

"It's your last night's milk, Nick," he pointed out. "All those cans came out of your cooler."

Shostikov felt each can. "That's right, Em. Maybe the cooler is fritzed."

Emery reported this incident at home.

"Was Nick sore?" asked his father with a worried look.

"No. He seemed to take it all right."

Shostikov didn't withdraw from the Co-op and his milk was all right the next morning. When Emery asked Mr. Rudnek about it, Sam replied: "Yesterday his cans—those three—were plain foul. They've never been like that before and today they're all right again. It's sure got me buffaloed."

Emery shook his head: that was one he couldn't figure.

A few days later, another member's milk was rejected and he pulled out of the Co-op. Bullock bought his one share of stock. Sam said: "His cans, half of them, showed bad cases of mastitis. What gets me is that they didn't show up before. And the A.D. won't take his milk if it's as bad as the cans he brought here."

But the A.D. did take him. No one could explain that. When the Cranes were discussing this at supper, David spoke up: "If they'd let me check up on the Co-op herds, this could all be fixed up. Old Spivac's to blame. You're letting him run the Co-op into the ground."

The rest of the family ignored him.

Emery hadn't seen Mary to talk to lately. Her father was delivering the milk alone, and he didn't seem to talk to anyone. Some of the members were saying that Jack was getting mighty hard to deal with. Others just shook their heads: they reckoned Spivac was having too many troubles.

One afternoon while Emery was cutting the upper field of alfalfa, he noticed that the Spivacs were putting up their crop already cut. He thought it didn't look sufficiently cured to put in the barn—it might heat up, cause internal combustion, and burn the barn down. But he recalled that the weather report at noon had predicted rain for tomorrow, so he concluded that Spivac had decided to take a chance.

That evening Mr. Crane came home from Sheltonville where he had gone to make payments on his bank debts and to arrange for a loan so that he could buy the Reilly share of Co-op stock.

"How'd you make out, Dad?" Emery asked.

"I can get the loan. Haley seemed quite friendly."

"I wonder—is that good or bad?"

"Don't see any catch to it now. We'll have to pay up in March; that's when our big test comes."

They started the milking and said no more about it.

Chapter Seventeen

FIRE

Bets started her nurse's training in the Utica Hospital the first of the month. Because of this expense, Mrs. Crane hadn't mentioned getting water piped into the house before winter. However, Emery and his father discussed it when they were in the fields. Everything hinged on the condition of the Co-op. If more milk had to be rejected and more members withdrew, they'd have to forget that project.

The second Monday in September, George Kressel's milk was rejected and when Emery reported this at dinner,

David said: "Yeah. George told me when he met me up at the mailboxes at the crossroads."

"Did he act sore?" asked Mr. Crane anxiously.

"Not at the Co-op anyhow," answered David.

At milking time, David wasn't around and when Emery asked about him, Mr. Crane said: "He wanted to be let off this evening. I thought it would be all right."

"What's he up to?" asked Emery.

"He didn't say."

David didn't come home for supper and Mr. Crane remarked: "I thought he'd be home to eat anyhow."

Emery thought back over the afternoon to see if he could find some clue to his brother's mysterious behavior. The two of them had been repairing fence on the ridge above the house; they had looked across the fields and had seen Spivac repairing his silo.

"Hope old Spivac falls in it," David had griped. "Him and his get-tough stand at the Co-op is driving members away. Bet he's just doing it on Muller's orders."

"You're talking crazy," Emery had retorted.

"Bet he is. Want to bet?"

That was the only scrap of talk Emery could remember, and that didn't add up to a reason for David's disappearance.

After supper Emery brought his account books up to date. He figured that when his next milk check came through he would have enough saved to buy his sixth cow. Two more and he'd have eight and be set to rent the Armstrong place. Once he thought of Mary; he hadn't seen her for a couple of weeks. Her father brought the milk down regularly himself now.

The telephone, ringing the general alarm, interrupted Emery's thoughts. His mother listened to the call, then cried: "The Spivacs' barn's on fire!"

Emery leaped out of his chair. "Come on! We've got to get over there."

His parents followed him out to the car and they started for the Spivacs'. As the machine topped the hill north, they all gasped; before them lay the Spivac yard completely dominated by the roaring fury of the burning barn. A number of cars were already there and more were arriving.

Emery couldn't take his eyes off the swirling, leaping flames that rose a hundred feet into the night, hurling up a whitish-gray cloud of smoke. Sparks showered down on all sides and the intense heat felt like a weight against his face.

The Cranes joined a crowd by the gate and Mr. Crane asked: "Jack get his cows out all right?"

"They're out," replied Nels Peterson.

Emery saw the Atlas Volunteer Fire Company Truck in the center of the yard, the firemen playing water on the machine shed and chickenhouses. He looked around for Mary but didn't see her. Her father and mother and several of her younger brothers and sisters were over at the pump house. He saw Jim Lane and his wife with them there.

More neighbors drove up. "How'd it start?" someone asked.

"Nobody knows. It just started."

"Maybe it was a short in the wiring."

Emery remembered the hay he had seen the Spivacs making last week—maybe it *had* been too green.

A yell went up: "Look at the house!" And Emery saw a flame flickering on the shingles. The crowd broke into action. "Get a ladder! Get some water."

Emery helped Nels Peterson steady a ladder against the house, then climbed up to the roof. The flame in the wood shingles burned merrily as if it meant no harm. Emery's hand trembled as he reached for the pail of water handed him and slopped it over the orange tongue. It hissed out. He splashed the rest of the water on the roof, wetting it down.

The fire in the barn had reached the end near the house and the heat was terrific. Sparks and burning bits came down like rain. Another flame started in the house roof and Emery sloshed it out.

"Hey, Em, is it hot up there?" called Chuck Lane from the top of the ladder.

"Sure is." Emery's face felt parched and his clothes were soaked with sweat.

"Let me take over for a spell," Chuck offered.

"Okay." Emery gave up his spot on the roof. When he climbed down and stumbled away from the foot of the ladder he almost bumped into Mary and Del Bunce.

"Is the house safe, Em?" asked Mary anxiously.

"Sure." Then he added: "Sorry about your barn, Mary." He wondered how Bunce happened to be here.

"When I get a dairy," Del boasted, "I'm going to have it equipped with an automatic fire-fighting system."

"When you get a dairy!" Emery snorted sarcastically. The heat from the burning barn and the presence of young Bunce seemed to combine to make him mad. "You'll never be anything but a stooge for Muller."

"I'm going to have a dairy all right," Del Bunce replied evenly, "and I won't be stooging for Muller either."

Emery gave a short, derisive laugh, but he saw a look of determination in Bunce's face which he had never noticed there before.

Mary interrupted: "This'll ruin us. Only the barn was insured, not the hay. We'll have nothing to feed our cows this winter."

"Find out who started the fire and you can get damages," Bunce pointed out.

"Who started the fire!" Mary cried. "Nobody started it. Who'd want to burn our barn?"

"Maybe several people," Bunce went on with a sly insinuating tone. "I could name several."

Mary turned on him angrily. "Don't try to make trouble. Dad said it was a short in the electric wiring."

"Maybe." Bunce looked wise and turned to Emery, "Hey, Crane, where's your kid brother? He come with you?"

"Home, I guess," Emery grunted.

"Thought I met him on the road near here," Bunce continued. "He ducked into a hedgerow like a scared rabbit."

Emery was reminded of David's strange absence this evening.

Bunce said: "Guess your kid brother was plenty sore at Mr. Spivac for chasing him out of the Co-op so that he couldn't make trouble with the microscope."

How did Bunce know about that, Emery wondered;

then he began to realize what Bunce meant by his sly talk.

"What're you hinting at?" he demanded.

"Why nothing at all," Bunce answered, sneering.

Emery's arm muscles tightened and his fists clenched.

"Stop it, you two," Mary said sharply. "You shut up, Del. Don't start a lot of mean talk you can't prove."

Bunce went on grinning smugly and Emery turned back to watch the fire. Almost all the wooden walls of the barn had burned. Only the huge pile of burning hay remained, black against the flames still leaping from the crest. Patches of red glowed on the sides where the fire ate into the mass.

"Let's watch from my car, Mary," Bunce suggested.

Emery hoped that she would refuse to go with him but when he glanced around a little later both were gone. Immediately his anger at Bunce whipped up again: what'd he mean by insinuating that David had set fire to the Spivac barn? But where was Dave tonight anyhow?

The fire had burned low enough so that Chuck Lane could come down off the house roof, and Emery and he joined a group of dairymen talking around Jack Spivac.

Jim Lane was saying: "Lou Crane and I'll stay with Jack to keep tabs on the fire. Chuck and Em can take our folks home." Then he turned to George Kressel. "How about letting Jack drive his cows over to your barn in the morning at milking time, George? Yours is the closest."

"Sure," agreed Kressel readily. "Bring 'em over."

"Thanks," Spivac replied weakly.

When Emery and his mother got home they saw a light in the house and David was waiting for them.

"Where've you been?" he asked at once.

"Where've *you* been, I'd like to know?" Emery demanded.

"I've been home for three hours. Did you go to the movies?" David looked hurt because he'd missed going with them.

"Spivac's barn burned down," explained his mother.

"Spivac's barn?" David's mouth hung open.

"Yes," snapped Emery. "Where were you tonight anyhow?"

David looked shaken. "I was here after eight-thirty."

"Before that," Emery insisted.

"I—I . . ." A defiant look came into the boy's face. "It's none of your business."

"It *is* my business!"

Mrs. Crane said: "You two had better get to bed. Your father won't be home until late and you'll have to get up and do the milking in the morning."

"I want to know what Dave was doing tonight," Emery said stubbornly. "It's important." He regretted adding that because he didn't want his mother to know of his suspicion.

"It's not that important," said their mother. "Now both of you go to bed at once."

Emery went upstairs, telling himself that he'd get Dave down to the barn in the morning and make him tell what he'd been up to. He'd make him talk! As if to hurry that opportunity along, he flung himself into bed.

ONE MYSTERY SOLVED

But in the morning at milking time, David still refused to tell what he'd been doing the previous evening.

"Look, Dave," Emery appealed to him, "you'd better open up and tell so we can help you out of a jam."

"I'm not in any jam," David replied.

"Oh no? It looks as if you fired Spivac's barn!"

The boy blinked as if he'd been hit; then he said thickly: "I—I didn't do anything of the kind."

"It looks like it—you keeping so mum. And Del Bunce saw you on the road."

"I didn't set anybody's barn on fire," David insisted indignantly now. "What I was doing is my business."

Emery gave up in disgust: how could he help the kid if he wouldn't tell him what he'd been up to?

At the Co-op station Emery overheard Peterson, Carsen, and Shostikov talking about the Spivac fire.

"I saw Jack taking up some mighty green alfalfa before it rained last week," Carsen said.

Then Peterson made some remark and all three looked quickly toward Emery. He pretended he hadn't noticed, but he wondered if they'd tied David to the burning of Spivac's barn? Was that story spreading already?

All the anger he'd felt at his brother vanished suddenly. He told himself that if David was accused, he'd testify that he'd seen Jack Spivac taking up green hay. Homer Carsen had seen that too, he'd just said so.

As he passed the Spivac dairy on the way home, he noticed Mr. Muller and Del Bunce talking to the Spivacs. They were at the back porch of the house staring down at the black smoking pile of hay where the barn had stood. What business did Muller and Del Bunce have there, Emery wondered.

He decided he'd better tell his dad about David; they had to figure out some way to defend the kid. But when he got home he found that Mr. Crane was still asleep, catching up for last night's watch at the fire. David had started trimming the hedgerow along the road and Emery went to help him.

"Any milk rejected this morning?" David asked.

"Not that I saw or heard of," Emery replied.

They cut and whacked at the wild growth of brush along the road. A car came down from the north and braked to a stop. Jack Spivac climbed out.

"Morning," Emery said. He noticed that David looked scared.

Spivac ignored Emery and turned on his brother: "Where were you last evening?"

"I—I can't say," David stammered.

"Del Bunce saw you on the road near my place." The dairyman's voice was thick with anger. "You've been sore at me ever since we chased you out of the Co-op station. You decided to get even with me and set my barn on fire."

"I didn't." David looked helplessly around.

"That alfalfa you put up was kind of green," Emery suggested to Spivac.

"It wasn't the hay that started that fire," the dairyman growled. "I know when hay's ready to put up."

"It could have been a shorted wire," Emery added.

"It was this kid trying to get even with me for stopping him fooling around at the Station." Spivac shook a fist at the boy. "I'm going to have you arrested. We aren't going to tolerate firebugs around here."

Mr. Crane, coming down to help with the hedge trimming, stepped through the row at that moment. "What's the trouble?" he demanded.

"Your kid here set my barn on fire," yelled Spivac.

"You're a big liar!" David yelled back.

"What're you talking about?" Mr. Crane looked confused. "David didn't set your barn on fire, Jack."

"He was seen near my place," stormed Spivac. "He's been wanting to get back at me."

Mr. Crane took a solid breath. "What were you up to last night, Dave?"

"I didn't burn his old barn." The boy swallowed hard. "That's all I can tell you."

"See!" shouted Spivac. "If he wasn't up to some mischief like setting my barn on fire, then he could tell you. He did it and I'm going to get the sheriff."

"No you're not!" Mr. Crane jumped down the bank. "If Dave says he didn't set fire to your barn, then he didn't."

"He'll have to prove it in court." Spivac shook both fists in the air.

A truck stopped beside them and George Kressel got out. "I didn't take your cans over to your place, Jack," he said, "because you'll still be milking in my barn." He seemed to notice the circle of angry faces, and hesitated before turning to David: "My last night's milk was rejected, Dave."

The brush-hook dropped from the boy's hands. "No! It was all right. We tested . . ." He broke off suddenly.

"It smelled at the station," Kressel continued. "Sam made slides and checked. It was bad—very bad."

David gulped. "It couldn't have been. You and Sam saw the slides I made—you checked them yourself."

"According to your slides," Kressel said, "every one of my cows is clear. But that wasn't what showed on the slides for those four cans of milk this morning."

"I took those smears right, honestly," David insisted.

Kressel laughed. "We're not doubting you, Dave. The point is, those four cans of milk were fouled after you took the smears. Somebody's been fixing my milk so it'll be rejected. Maybe that's what's been happening to other Co-op members' milk so they'll get sore and pull out. Your slides proved my cows were all right. But this morning my milk was foul and I mean foul!"

Mr. Crane interrupted: "What's this about Dave making slides?"

Kressel explained: "After my milk was rejected yesterday morning, I figured I ought to have my cows tested, so I met Dave at the mailboxes and asked him to come over at milking time and take smears."

"He could still have set my barn on fire on the way home," Spivac broke in.

"Don't be a darned fool!" Kressel told him. "I let Dave off at the corner just half an hour before I heard about your fire and by that time the whole middle of your barn was blazing. He couldn't have set it on fire, and you know it. Besides Dave wouldn't do a trick like that and you know that too."

Mr. Crane turned to David. "Why didn't you explain all this?"

"I—I wasn't supposed to make slides or go near the Co-op or the microscope. I was afraid you'd give me . . . Well, anyhow, the Co-op's been having enough trouble lately."

"I think the Co-op had better hire Dave as a special tester," Kressel suggested.

Spivac got into his car suddenly and drove off without saying another word.

David groaned: "He still thinks I burned his barn."

"He's crazy," Kressel said. "Guess Jack's in a tight spot. Only enough insurance to build a new barn, not enough to buy hay for winter. The bank and Muller have him hog-tied." He squinted thoughtfully. "Might have been Muller who put him up to accusing Dave, to cause a split among us."

Emery remembered Del Bunce's insinuation last night, and Bunce and Muller were at Spivac's already this morning.

"I can't figure what happened to your milk," said Mr. Crane.

"It was fouled in the cooler. That's how I figure it," Kressel replied.

"I'll bet that's what happened," Emery spoke up. "I helped Nick Shostikov load his rejected milk one morning —it was all cooler milk. We noticed it at the time."

"Guess the Co-op members had better start locking their coolers," said Mr. Crane.

Kressel handed David two one-dollar bills. "Here, Dave, that's for the job you did last night."

"Aw, I don't want to be paid." The boy drew back.

"Take it. You earned it." Kressel pushed the money into his hands.

David saw his father grin and his fingers closed over the money. "Thanks. Gee, thanks."

That noon Mr. Crane called up the Co-op directors and asked them to meet with him at the station after supper. Emery, waiting up for him, heard him drive into the yard. But when Mr. Crane didn't come to the house at once, Emery looked out the window and saw the lights on in the milkhouse.

"What were you doing in the milkhouse, Dad?" Emery asked, when his father finally came into the living room.

"Making sure the cooler was locked."

"What happened at the meeting?"

"We decided to notify all Co-op patrons to put locks on their coolers," replied Mr. Crane. "Charlie Bullock said we were crazy and voted against it. Spivac wasn't there." Then he added: "Del Bunce's car was at the Spivacs' when I went down. It was gone when I came home."

A sudden wild suspicion jolted Emery to his toes: Del Bunce had been in the neighborhood a lot lately; had he been sneaking into milkhouses and fouling the milk of Co-op members, doing it for the A.D. or Muller?

He bit his lip. Locking the coolers would put a stop to such tricks, he assured himself, and unless they caught Bunce in the act, they couldn't prove anything against him.

Chapter Nineteen

CO-OPERATION

The next morning Milt Barrett's cooler milk was bad and Sam rejected it. Milt got mad but when Sam explained what George Kressel had discovered Milt understood. "It's somebody from the A.D. who's doing it," he growled.

And after the Co-op patrons began locking their coolers, no more bad milk came in. George Kressel got up a petition asking the directors to reinstate David Crane at the job of helping Rudnek with the bacteria records and to pay him for his work. "Gee," David said, "maybe I can save up enough money to buy a microscope of my own."

On the way home from delivering the milk one

morning, Emery saw lumber piled in the Spivac yard, and masons had started pouring the foundation and floor for a new barn.

When he reported this at home, his father said: "Jack's getting a new barn, but his problem will be to fill it with hay."

Emery hadn't seen the Spivacs lately. And nothing more was said about the cause of the fire. But one evening, when the truck garden season had ended, Walter Longstreth came over to say good-bye, and he mentioned it.

"Someone started the story around Sheltonville that one of us migrants set the fire," Walter said. "You see Muller's supposed to transport us back south—that's part of his contract with us. I guess he figured that by working up that story he might scare us into pulling out."

"Well, of all the mean tricks," said Mrs. Crane.

Walter chuckled. "We didn't scare that easily. Tomorrow morning Muller's taking all the migrants but me back south. I'm heading west."

In answer to the Cranes' quick question: "Why west?" he explained that he was going out to Ann Arbor, Michigan to enter the University. They all wished him luck and invited him to come to see them again; then Emery drove him back to the vicinity of the Muller farm.

When he returned past the Spivac place, he heard pounding and saw a bright glow: the carpenters were working under floodlights, rushing the job. After that, he marked the progress of the new barn every day. The morning he noticed that the roof was on, he saw the Spivac pickup truck in the station yard, and knew that the Spivacs were milking at home again. He wondered who had brought their milk this morning, Mary or her father. It was Mary who climbed out to unload.

Emery hurried to help her. She seemed a little shy.

"Haven't seen you lately, Em."

"I've been around." He tried to sound offhand.

Her face flushed a little. "I'm sorry about Dad picking on Dave," she said softly. "But he's having so much trouble lately he flies off the handle at almost anything."

"Forget it," Emery said; then he asked: "Coming to the Co-op picnic at the Fair next week, Mary?"

"I don't know." She looked away. "We're so busy."

"Gee, hope you can come . . ."

He didn't see Mary at the station during the next few days, but he hoped to see her at the Co-op picnic. The night before that big day at the Morris Springs Fair, Jim Lane stopped at the Cranes' to talk over some final details in the program with Mr. Crane.

When Jack Spivac was mentioned, Jim Lane asked: "What's Jack doing about winter hay?"

Mr. Crane shook his head.

But Emery spoke up: "I think the Co-op ought to help him out. If each member gave a load or two, he'd have enough."

"Muller and the bank are squeezing Jack hard," Jim Lane said. The Co-op might help him through." But nothing more was said about it at the time, and Lane drove off home, saying: "See you at the fair grounds."

The Co-op members and their families numbered over two hundred when they assembled in a shady corner of the Morris Springs Fair Grounds for their picnic dinner.

But the Spivacs didn't come. Emery was disappointed: maybe they'd come for the afternoon. That hope made him restless while listening to the talks that followed the picnic dinner.

Percy Woods warned the members to look out for more tricks from the A.D. "Harvey Bunce has been on the pan several times lately," he told them. "The big producers are getting tired of taking the short end of the butterfat record so that the small dairymen they still have as patrons can be kept happy. They'd like nothing better than to see the Co-op licked and return to the good old days when they took the lions' share of the butterfat and you small dairymen took the cut."

"They're not going to lick us, Percy!" yelled Harold Shontz, and the crowd gave a shout of agreement.

Jim Lane made a report on the present condition of the Co-op. It was solid. Thanks to Charlie Bullock, who now held more than twenty shares, all turned-in stock had been bought up promptly.

Bullock received loud applause from the crowd and shouts of: "Stand up, Charlie, take a bow," but he remained seated, his square face red, his eyes fixed on the ground.

Then Jim Lane continued: "We've got to stick together to win our fight against the A.D. Any serious misfortune that weakens any member can weaken all of us as a group. You all know that Jack Spivac suffered considerable loss in his recent fire. He was insured to cover the loss of his barn, but not the hay in it. Yesterday, Co-operator Emery Crane suggested that every Co-op mem-

ber who could spare some hay should give it to Jack. I
think that was a mighty good suggestion. What do you
think about it?"

The crowd was silent a moment, then a cheer went up.
Emery's face burned.

"I suggest that as soon as we adjourn," Lane concluded, "every member who can spare Spivac some hay
come up here and put down the number of loads he can
give."

After the meeting the dairymen gathered at one of
the picnic tables to sign up. In a short time the Spivacs
had the promise of almost a hundred loads of hay.

Emery and Chuck Lane went to see the sights along
the Midway and Emery had the uncomfortable feeling
that now he was glad Mary hadn't come. Gee, how
could he face her now that Jim Lane had told that he'd
suggested the hay pool for her father?

That evening the Co-op dairymen went home to milk
their herds, feeling that it had been a successful day. And
Emery, confident that the Co-op was solid, began to plan
again. As soon as he got three more cows, he would rent
the Armstrong place and start on his own.

The next few mornings he missed seeing Mary at the
station. He wanted to see her, but suppose she'd heard
about the hay pool for her father; what might she say,
or do, or think. Darn Jim Lane for telling where the idea
came from!

Tuesday when he turned south toward home from
Route 20, he noticed that carpenters were putting a new
roof on the old Livermore barn. The Livermore place was

a big abandoned farm and Emery wondered briefly who was taking it over. He was in a hurry and it soon slipped his mind.

That morning they were starting to fill silo. The silage cutter was set and the neighbors—the Lanes, Nels Peterson, and Harold Shontz—had arrived to help with the job by the time he got home. At dinner that noon, Nels Peterson remarked that the dairymen planned to start today to haul the hay they had promised Jack Spivac.

Emery blushed at the mention of it and hurried back to driving the tractor and cornbinder in the field, cutting the green corn for the haulers to take up to the cutter. Once when he swung the tractor at the end of the field, he glanced up to see Mary riding Dolly across the stubble toward him. He throttled down.

"Hi, Mary," he said, trying to act nonchalant as she rode up beside the big rubber-tired tractor wheel, but his fingers fiddled nervously with the levers.

"Nick Shostikov and Hans Overgaard brought over four loads of hay today," she said, her blue eyes watching him intently. "They said it was your idea, Em."

"Oh—uh." He bogged down. "Somebody else would have thought of it if I hadn't."

"I came over to thank you for us." Her glance slid down to the corn stubble. "I don't know if Dad'll ever thank you for it. He's so beaten . . . He's been saying that next March he's going to let the bank and Muller take everything."

"Oh." Emery's face twisted. "He can't, Mary. What'll he do if he gives up the dairy?"

"We'll move to Atlas or Sheltonville." She bit her lip before continuing: "He didn't want to take the hay, but Hans said it was better than a snowbank to feed the cows. Dad says he'll pay each one back some day. Anyhow, it'll save us from having to borrow more money."

Emery tried to think of something to say, but couldn't.

After patting Dolly's neck, Mary said: "I wanted you to know we appreciate your promoting the hay pool, Em, even if Dad never gets around to telling you himself."

"Aw, I didn't do anything." He gave a hard yank at the steering wheel in an attempt to break up the confusion he felt; then he blurted out: "Say, Mary, how about . . ." His face grew redder than ever. How could he ask Mary to go to the movies with him when she and her folks thought they owed him something over the hay pool idea? Doggone Jim Lane!

"What?" She watched him closely and a little smile twitched the corners of her mouth. "There's a good movie on in Sheltonville Saturday night," she said.

His jaw champed but he couldn't say anything for a moment. "You—you wouldn't think I was . . ." He didn't finish.

"No." Her smile broadened; her eyes began to twinkle.

"Will you, Mary?" He almost yelled the question.

She nodded.

"Saturday night?"

Again she nodded. "I have to go home now. See you Saturday." She turned Dolly and galloped out of the field.

Emery's recent violent embarrassment changed now

to wild exuberance. He sent the tractor recklessly down the field until the cornbinder threw the drive chain. Then he stopped, sobered down, fixed the chain, and resumed cutting at normal speed, whistling loudly into the clatter of the rig.

Chapter Twenty

THE COWS COME HOME

Thick frost covered the hills and valleys of central New York in the mornings now and the sun felt good when it came up. It wouldn't be long before the dairymen brought their herds in from pasture and kept them in the barns.

The first Friday in October Mr. Crane brought Bets home from Utica for her first weekend holiday since she had begun her nurse's training at the hospital there.

When Emery came downstairs Saturday night dressed up in his best clothes, she said, with a smirk, "Oh hooo." Then with raised eyebrows, she asked: "Mary?"

"Who else?" David answered for his brother.

"Go stare in your microscope," Emery told him.

"Would if I had one." Then David puffed out his chest. "David Crane, Expert Milk Analyst. Like that?"

"How much have you saved toward buying a microscope, Dave?" asked his sister.

"Seventy-five dollars. They cost too much."

Bets turned to Emery, and straightened his coat collar. "Guess you look like a promising young dairyman."

"Don't promise too much," David teased.

"That's enough out of you, microbe hunter," Emery said.

"When are you starting your dairy, Em?" asked Bets.

He held up three fingers. "Three more cows. I have money to buy one right now."

When he arrived at the Spivacs', Mrs. Spivac invited him in. The three younger children giggled, and Conrad twitched his crooked shoulders, while his eyes twinkled.

"Better bring me home some candy, Em," he said, "or I won't be on your side with Mary."

"I'll do that," Emery agreed, grinning, but his hands felt too big for his pockets.

Mr. Spivac looked up from his paper. "Get your silo filled, Em?"

"Day before yesterday." Then, fearing that Spivac might say something about the hay pool, he hurried on: "Know anybody who has a good cow to sell?"

The dairyman's eyes tightened thoughtfully. "Mary has one that'll freshen in March. Maybe she'll sell."

Mary, coming downstairs at that moment, overheard and said quickly: "I don't want to sell Ivy, Dad."

"Just have to feed her for six months."

"But I raised her—I won a 4H club prize with her," Mary said; then with a quick smile at Emery, "Guess I'm ready."

He found it hard to talk as they drove to Sheltonville. When they met at the Co-op station it hadn't been difficult, but now his tongue seemed tied in a knot.

"The—the moon's bright," he stammered.

"Yes." She didn't seem to find it easy to talk either.

The stiffness between them didn't matter while they sat through the movie, but in the drugstore after the show the knot in his tongue bothered him again while they waited for their ice cream to be served. She sat across from him, smiling, her eyes sparkling, her cheeks full of color. Now he ought to say, "Gee, Mary, you're pretty," but the words jammed up in his throat and wouldn't come out.

But the pressure to say something was strong. "Mary —I—I'd sure like to buy that heifer." His tongue loosened. "I want to get my herd built up—eight more cows giving milk by spring—then I'm going to rent the Armstrong place."

A sudden feeling of embarrassment stopped him.

"Dad's been after me to sell Ivy . . ." The waitress brought their order and she became preoccupied with her spoon.

"I know how you feel about her," he said hurriedly. "But if you sold her you—you could help . . ."

"Yes, Dad could use the money all right." The corners of her mouth tightened.

"It would be your money, I mean." Gee, maybe he'd

hurt her feelings. He was a dope to bring up this subject, he told himself, and looked across the store feeling dejected.

Del Bunce was just skirting a table, coming toward their booth, carrying a dish of ice cream.

"Hi, Mary. Mind if I join you?" He sat down beside her without an invitation, ignoring Emery. "Have you noticed what's been happening at the old Livermore place?" he asked. "It's my pitch. I'm on my own. Twenty head of milkers beginning the first of the year."

"Wonderful, Del," said Mary eagerly.

Emery, studying Bunce's face, saw that the pudginess was gone from his cheeks. "Muller putting up the cash?" he asked stiffly.

"That's right. Old J. Holland Muller's setting me up."

"Then you're not on your own," Emery retorted. "You're still a stooge for Muller."

Bunce glared across the table. "Get this straight, Crane. I said I'd be on my own and I mean *on my own.*"

"If Muller puts up the cash, he'll give the orders. And if he tells you to put foul milk in Co-op members' cooler milk, you'll do it or else." Emery flung the accusation recklessly.

Bunce reddened and he half rose, fists clenched.

"Stop it, you two," Mary ordered. "Eat your ice cream."

An embarrassed silence followed; then Bunce continued: "I told Muller I thought the Co-op was a good idea and I'm going to buy stock. Does that make me Muller's stooge?"

"Sure," snapped Emery.

"Stop it, Em!" Mary said sharply.

Bunce stood up. "Guess I'd better run along before this conversation gets rough." He walked stiffly away.

"I still say he's Muller's stooge," muttered Emery.

"But he's going to buy Co-op stock," insisted Mary.

"He's just talking big."

Emery was mad at himself because he couldn't help envying Del Bunce for being able to start out with twenty cows, while he had to wait until he got three more and then he'd have only eight to start with. They started home and he again found it hard to make conversation. But as they neared Atlas, Mary whispered: "Em, I'll sell you Ivy."

"Gee, Mary, swell. But—if you don't want to sell her— I mean . . ."

"I've changed my mind, Em." She glanced up at him, laughing as she added: "If I sell her to you, I can come and see her some time, can't I?"

"Sure. Any time." He suddenly felt good-natured again. "Gee, now when I get two more cows I can start dickering for the Armstrong place." But after a pause he added: "Won't be like starting with twenty milkers though."

"You won't be taking orders from Muller anyhow," replied Mary bitterly, and Emery wondered if she was thinking about the spot her father was in.

Back at the Spivacs', Emery walked with Mary up to the house, the light of the full moon bright around them. From the distance came the sound of baying hounds.

"They're running a fox," he whispered as the bellowing of the dogs grew in the clear frosty air. "They're down near Lane's." Emery followed the course of the fox. "He's swinging over toward our place now," he said. "He's crossing the road, heading west. He's sure giving them a run tonight. Must be cutting through Kressel's sugarbush about now and, from the sound, he's swinging back this way."

Mary shivered. Then suddenly across the yard before them flashed a long, slim shape. The animal's brush flowed out behind it like a wave.

"He's heading for your cattleyard," Emery predicted.

Mary clutched his arm as the hounds roared past. They leaped the barnyard fence, then abruptly grew quiet. The trail of the fox was lost in the stronger barnyard smells.

"I hope he gets away." Mary's teeth were chattering.

Then the baying started up from beyond the yard.

"They've picked it up again," said Emery, but almost at once the bellowing of the hounds ceased. "They've lost it. I'll bet he swam your pond. They've lost it for good."

The night grew quiet, and the frost gleamed on the new barn roof like metal.

"I'll come over some time next week and get your cow," Emery said. "Will that be all right?"

"Sure. Thanks for a good time, Em. Good night."

She went quietly indoors.

Emery drove on home, thinking: let Bunce start with his twenty milkers, I don't care; I may be starting out in a slow way but I won't be in debt.

Dark gray clouds hung low in the sky when he brought Mary's big black and white Holstein down to his father's barn. The next night one of the heifers he had bought from Kressel lagged behind coming up from the pasture. He put her in a stall by herself and bedded her down with straw.

"She look all right to you, Dad?" he asked Mr. Crane.

"She'll be all right," his father assured him.

The next morning he sprang out of bed in his cold room and from habit glanced out of the window immediately. The pre-dawn darkness seemed strangely gray-white and he realized that it was snowing. Then his father turned on the yard light; it exploded in the whiteness. He heard a door slam; then he saw his father start down to the barn, leaving slowly disappearing tracks behind him.

Emery remembered his heifer: had she had her calf yet? He hurried into his clothes and followed his father. The barn, warmed by the body heat of the cows, was more comfortable than the still cold house. Emery found the heifer chewing her cud, and a new calf lay curled up beside her.

"From the looks of that cow's bag," remarked Mr. Crane, "you'll soon be adding a lot more milk to your cans."

Emery scratched the cow's black glossy ear. She belched up a fresh cud and began to chew. "Guess the cows stay in today," he remarked to his father.

"Yes. The cows came home last night to stay," replied Mr. Crane. "Right here they'll stay until grass time again."

They began the milking and Emery thought: "Grass time." By then he'd have eight cows and his own dairy. Well, that was something to dream about anyhow.

Chapter Twenty-one

GOALS REACHED

The first snow melted in a few days; then came a week of Indian Summer. On these fine days, after the dairy was cleaned in the morning and the manure hauled to the fields, Emery and his father worked at installing the water system into the house. The apparent solidness of the Co-op convinced Mr. Crane that they could risk the added expense, and the job was finished just before Thanksgiving.

"This is certainly something to be thankful for," said Mrs. Crane, turning the tap at the kitchen sink.

156

Bets came home for the holiday. "Running water," she said, "just like the city now."

But David groused: "Bets gets to be a nurse, Mom gets running water, Em gets more cows, but I don't get anything."

"Christmas isn't here yet," said his mother, and he didn't do any more complaining.

Emery saw Mr. Spivac regularly at the Co-op station but the dairyman hardly did more than nod to him. He overheard neighbors gossiping: "It's darned rough the way Muller and the bank have their hands around Jack's neck. He's just about licked." Mary seldom came along with her father these winter mornings, but one morning, when she did, Emery went to talk with her, and she asked with a laugh: "How's Ivy?"

"Fine. When are you coming over to see her?"

"Think she misses me, Em?"

"Sure she does. She mentioned it just yesterday." They both laughed, and he asked her to go to the movies.

"Dad doesn't want me to go out with you, Em," she said, but she didn't look at him.

"Is he sore at me for something, Mary?"

"It isn't that." She looked unhappy; then added: "Let's not talk about it, Em."

"All right," he agreed, but he couldn't understand it.

Right after the first of December, winter came down with all its fury and left the country piled high with snow. The temperature dropped below zero. Truck tires creaked on the snow-packed roads. Steam clouded up

from the dairy, the milkhouse, the Co-op station, and the
breaths of the dairymen. The sky, the air, and the land all
seemed steel-hard.

The second heifer Emery bought from Kressel freshened and he was now milking five cows; he was on the
look-out for two more. One evening Mr. Crane announced that Jerry Palmer wanted to sell two of his three
Co-op shares. "He needs some quick cash," Mr. Crane explained.

Emery went to see Palmer. "Do you have a cow you
want to sell?"

"I'm short of money," Palmer replied. "If I sell a cow
to get money, then I'll be short of cows."

"I'm looking for one that'll freshen in two or three
months," explained Emery.

Palmer scratched his stubbly chin. "I have one that'll
freshen about grass time. Might sell her."

They entered the dairy and Palmer pointed out a thin
Holstein. She could stand a bit more fat, Emery thought.
They talked price, agreed on a figure, and the first sunny
afternoon that followed, Emery brought her over to his
father's barn. Now he had seven cows—one more to go . . .

But when Palmer kept the two shares of Co-op stock
he had offered to sell, Mr. Crane reported that Jack
Spivac and Charlie Bullock got mad about it. "They each
wanted to buy a share," Mr. Crane said.

"Where's Spivac getting money to buy more stock?"
asked Emery puzzled.

"That's a question that's bothering more than you,"
replied his father.

One morning a week later, Emery saw Del Bunce at the Co-op station.

"Hi, Em," Del greeted him, coming over to his truck. "I hear you're looking for another cow."

"Yes." Emery felt himself stiffen witth suspicion.

"A dairyman over at Morris Springs is selling some young stock," Bunce informed him. "I'd be interested myself, except that I already have my twenty head."

"Thanks." But the suspicion showed in Emery's face.

"I'm giving you straight stuff," Bunce insisted. Then he added: "Come up and see my dairy, Em. It's a honey." His voice was full of pride. "I'll be all set to move in and start right after the first of the year."

"I'll drop in some time," said Emery, not meaning it.

Del started to go, then swung back. "Still think I'm stooging for Muller, don't you, Em?"

Emery hesitated, then said slowly: "Yes."

He expected Bunce to flare up; instead he only looked a little hurt. "Okay. Some day I'll show you that I'm not."

It was Mr. Crane who told Emery why Del Bunce had been at the Co-op. He came to buy ten shares of stock.

"Ten shares!" Emery yelled. "A thousand dollars worth? What's the idea of wanting that much?"

Mr. Crane shrugged, then went on to explain the real problem that had come up. Jim Lane and he had wanted to buy up ten existing shares from the membership and re-sell them to Bunce. But Spivac and Bullock insisted that they issue new shares and the other directors supported them.

"We shouldn't have done it." Mr. Crane shook his head. "We're over-capitalizing the Co-op and that's dangerous."

Christmas approached and Emery asked Bets' advice about a present for Mary. She suggested a wool hood and scarf set and bought it for him in Utica. He didn't have the courage to take it to Mary, so he sent it through the mail.

At the Cranes', Christmas morning, David was probably the happiest. By the tree in the corner of the dining room stood a microscope beneath its polished bellglass. Bets had located this second-hand microscope through the hospital in Utica. The family had pooled the money they had planned to use to buy him presents with what he had saved up toward purchasing a microscope, and they were able to get it for him.

"Now I'm really going into the milk-analyzing business," he boasted.

Emery's present was a single-head milking machine which he took to the dairy at once to try out. It spurred his ambition to get his own dairy and he decided to look into Del Bunce's tip about the cows for sale over at Morris Springs.

That evening after the chores were done the family sat around the fireplace and Bets and David popped corn. They heard a knock on the door and Mary Spivac looked in, calling, "Merry Christmas."

"Take off your things and join us," invited Mrs. Crane.

"I can't stay," she said. "I just went for a walk and thought I'd stop in." She looked shyly at Emery.

He had noticed at once that she wore the gayly colored wool cap and scarf he'd sent her.

"Come on, Mary, and stay," Bets urged.

"Honestly, I can't." She looked worried. "My folks don't know where I went. I have to go right back."

Emery went for his sheepskin coat and galoshes.

"I'll walk back with you," he offered.

When they stepped out on the porch, she rubbed the end of the scarf against his cheeks. "Thanks," she whispered.

He hunted frantically for something to say and finally stammered: "Wan—want to see Ivy?"

She gave a little laugh. "I never did get over to see her, did I?"

"Come wish her 'Merry Christmas.'" They started down the path to the dairy.

The rich smell of cattle and cured hay greeted them when he opened the door and turned on the lights. "There she is."

Mary had already picked her out of the row of cows and going up beside her patted the animal's glossy curved neck. "Hello, Ivy, how are you?" The cow turned her head and mooed softly. "She recognized me, Em," said Mary happily.

"She says, 'Don't stay away so long next time,'" Emery replied with a chuckle.

They started up the road to the Spivacs', slipping and sliding along the icy wheel tracks, laughing when one or the other came close to falling. On top of the first hill, they stopped to rest.

"How's everything at home, Mary?" he asked. For a moment he thought she wasn't going to answer.

Then she whispered: "Terrible. Dad's so blue all the time. We don't know if he's going to keep the place or not. He doesn't even tell Mother. It's all Muller's fault. I hate him. He ordered Dad to buy one of those shares of Co-op stock Palmer wanted to sell, and when you bought Palmer's cow and Palmer didn't sell his stock, Muller gave Dad an awful talking-to. I heard it. I don't know why Dad put up with it. I'd have hit him . . ." She broke off despairingly.

"I wish I could do something," Emery muttered helplessly.

She didn't say anything more the rest of the way home. At the gate, she said: "Thanks for walking me home, Em." Then she ran across the yard to the house.

Emery returned home thoughtfully. How could Muller make Mr. Spivac buy Co-op stock? Was Muller putting up the money? He told his father and Mr. Crane frowned.

"Jack's in a tight spot all right," he said. "But what worries me is that the A.D. and the big producers are planning one more big try to wreck the Co-op. But I can't figure out their game. The thousand which Del Bunce paid in for new stock has already been applied on the main debt and by March we'll be able to declare a nice dividend. Once we can declare a dividend, the Co-op will be proven. So the A.D. has to break us within the next couple of months or we'll be too solid to budge."

Emery couldn't figure out the A.D.'s game either, but the threat of more trouble stayed in the back of his mind. The following day he drove over to Morris Springs and looked up Ralph Wade. The dairyman had a young cow Emery liked at a price he considered fair, and he bought it.

When he closed the stanchion in the home barn on this eighth cow in his herd, his chest felt over-full of air. He had eight cows now. He was set to rent the Armstrong place, he told himself; then he blew out his full chest of air with a feeling of pride and triumph.

EMERY CRANE, DAIRYMAN

Emery discovered that the Sheltonville bank handled the Armstrong estate, and he wasn't surprised when Mr. Haley said to him: "Sorry, Emery, that farm isn't for rent." The banker seemed to enjoy watching the disappointment grow in Emery's face, before he added: "It's for sale only."

"Oh." Emery half shrugged. He was sure he couldn't buy the place. Or could he? "What's the price, sir?"

"Thirty-five hundred. One thousand down and you can take ten years to pay the other twenty-five hundred."

Emery felt the banker's cunning eyes watching him.

"I couldn't raise a thousand for the down payment," he said.

Mr. Haley scratched his chin. "You're an enterprising young man, Emery. The bank would consider you a good risk. I understand you own eight cows; a chattel mortgage on them would secure the loan of a thousand for you."

"I'll have to think about it, sir," he said, and left the bank, telling himself that he couldn't mortgage his herd.

All the way home he felt as if he'd had the wind kicked out of him; the dream he'd built up for a year was suddenly gone. There were other places he could rent, but none were near home and he needed to rent a place near his folks so that he could live at home and also help his father when he was needed.

When he reported the situation to his father, Mr. Crane said: "We need more barn room. Every stanchion is full now and I've three heifers freshening in April. You need to get your cows out so there'll be room for mine."

"Maybe I could build a barn," Emery suggested.

"That would cost more than a thousand," replied Mr. Crane. "Besides, with our growing herds, we need more land too."

They were working up in the sugarbush, cutting dead wood and stacking it for the maple syrup fires in late February or early March. The blows of their axes rang through the crisp winter air as they continued their work.

Once, in a pause, Emery remarked wishfully: "Maybe I could buy the Armstrong place."

His father squinted through the thick stand of big sugar maples. "Suppose we figure a little," he said.

All the rest of the day they examined the possibilities and reached the conclusion that if Emery didn't put too much money into immediate improvements, if the Co-op remained solid and grew, and if he had reasonable luck with his herd, he could buy the Armstrong place and pay for it. When they did the evening chores, Mr. Crane said: "I think we can go down to the bank in the morning and talk business."

Emery's first feeling of excitement soon vanished. A fellow didn't buy a farm every day. He was about to buy a future home and a way to make a living the rest of his life, and he didn't feel like doing much talking that evening.

The next morning he and his father went to see Mr. Haley and he signed the purchase agreement. A week later, Mr. White, their lawyer, wrote him that the papers for closing the deal were ready for his signature. After delivering the milk the following day, he drove over to Sheltonville.

"How do you feel?" asked Mr. White as they started to the bank.

"A little scared," Emery admitted.

Mr. White laughed. "I think you'll handle it all right." Then he added: "Unless something happens to the Co-op."

Emery remembered that qualifying statement on the way home after closing the deal. But what could happen to the Co-op? It was solid; it was booming. The A.D.

didn't have a chance to break it now. He pushed such fears aside.

And the next time Mary brought the milk from her father's dairy down to the station, Emery hurried to help her unload, eager to tell her the news.

"How's everything?" he asked.

She took a deep breath. "I guess Dad's giving up the dairy the first of March."

"Oh." He couldn't talk about buying the Armstrong place now. "I'm sorry, Mary."

Del Bunce drove his truck into the line and yelled at him: "Hi, dairyman." He was grinning as he joined them. "You told Mary?" he asked.

"Told me what?" Mary demanded.

"Beside you," said Del, "stands Emery Crane, dairyman, the buyer of the Armstrong farm."

"Why, Emery! Did you buy it, really? That's wonderful." She clutched his hand impulsively and shook it.

"My congratulations, too," added Bunce.

Emery managed to mumble, "Thanks," but he wondered where Bunce had heard the news, from the bank or from Muller. And he couldn't believe that Bunce's friendliness was real.

Then Del said: "How about stopping on the way home to have a look at my dairy, Em?"

"Pretty busy . . ." He tried to evade the invitation.

"Del's got a wonderful place, Em," said Mary.

He flashed her a quick look: how did she know?

It was time to pull up in the line and he didn't get to talk with Mary again. On the way home, Bunce was ahead of him and stopped his truck at the corners.

"Come on up and see my place," Del called back.

Emery hesitated, then answered, "Okay," and followed him.

Bunce showed off his dairy proudly but without his usual conceit. The walls of the barn gleamed with new paint; all the equipment was new. His cows seemed to be in fine shape.

"This is okay," Emery said grudgingly. Then he remembered Bunce's boasting at the Spivac fire that his dairy would have automatic fire-fighting equipment. "Where's your sprinkler system? Thought you were going to install fire-fighting equipment."

Del flushed. "I'm in debt to Muller too much as it is." Then he added bitterly: "But I'm still not Muller's stooge the way you think I am."

Emery pondered the change that had come over Del Bunce these past couple of months. He had really behaved pretty decently lately. Yet Emery couldn't believe that Muller would let him get out from under his thumb; the big producers were trying to build chain dairies, and Bunce was obviously expected to be part of the Muller chain in spite of his belonging to the Co-op. And for a moment, Emery wondered if Del's membership in the Co-op might not be part of Muller's plan for expansion. The thought worried him, then slipped his mind.

Toward the end of February a thaw hit central New York State and the maple sap began to rise. The day Emery and his father set up the evaporating pan it rained and both of them got wet. The next day the weather cleared and while Mr. Crane delivered the milk and made arrangements at the Co-op to borrow against future milk checks to help meet his March first debt payments, Emery began tapping the big maple trees, hanging buckets to catch the dripping sap.

His father came home to announce that a meeting of the Co-op directors was being called for the third of March to discuss the possibility of issuing a dividend. A Co-op dividend would really set the Co-op solid among the small dairymen, and Emery wondered how much his share would amount to.

The next day they started the fire under the evaporating pan and the sap flowing the length of it. The air was full of acrid wood smoke. Mr. Crane sneezed and blamed it on the smoke; then his joints began aching and by noon he had a fever. By evening he went to bed with the flu.

That left the responsibility for the syrup fire to Emery and David. Chuck Lane came over to help at night, and one afternoon Mary stoked the fire while Emery brought in the sap. Mingled with the wood smoke now was the rich sweetness of thickening syrup. They tossed some of it into clean snow, where it stiffened into soft maple wax; then they ate it greedily. The first syrup of the season was always something special.

Once Emery remarked: "Come the first of March— three more days—and I move my cows over to my own dairy."

"I think that's swell, Em," Mary answered.

"Your Dad still planning to quit?" he asked.

"He hasn't talked about it lately," she said.

That evening after chores, just as Emery started to relieve David up at the sugar fire, Jim Lane stopped in.

"Spivac and Bullock got Carsen and Hollis to call the directors' meeting tonight instead of next week," he said. "They know you're sick, Lou; I don't see why there's such a rush."

Mr. Crane stirred weakly under the covers. "I can't figure it out either."

"Looks to me as if they're calling the meeting tonight because Dad can't be there," Emery said.

Jim Lane shook his head. "I'll find out their reason when I get there," he said. "By the way, Chuck will be over to help stoke the syrup fire at midnight."

The air was sharp up in the sugarbush; the moon, still low in the east, pushed the scraggly shadows of the big maples out across the field. Maybe, Emery thought, the directors want to declare the dividend before the first of March; it might help some of the dairymen out with their March first debt payments.

He tried to convince himself that this conclusion was right and stopped thinking about the problem for the moment. As he stoked up the fire under the evaporator and added more sap to the upper end of the long pan, he thought he heard voices and glanced toward the farm-yard. Two figures came running across the field in the moonlight. Fear gripped him: was his dad suddenly worse? Then he recognized them—Mary Spivac and Del Bunce.

"They're going to sell the Co-op, Em," Mary panted.

"Sell the Co-op!" The chill of the winter night seemed to cut through him suddenly. "They can't sell it! It can't be sold unless a majority of the members say so."

"But they are," cried Mary frantically.

Emery glanced suspiciously at Del Bunce. Was this a gag? He felt himself getting mad. "They can't sell it!" But the seriousness in Bunce's face was unquestionable. Emery didn't know what to do; he threw a stick on the fire.

"We'd better go talk to your dad, Em," Bunce said. "We'll tell you what's cooking as we go."

"Hurry, Em," urged Mary.

They started out of the sugarbush toward the house.

Chapter Twenty-three

THE FIGHT

When they reached the open field, Emery turned half around and asked: "Now, what's all this about?"

They continued along the path while Del Bunce replied: "Muller called me this evening and told me to dump my ten shares of Co-op stock back on the Co-op in the morning."

"Still a stooge for Muller," Emery flung the accusation over his shoulder bitterly.

"Emery, you make me mad," Mary cried.

"He told me to dump my shares," Del continued, "but that doesn't mean that I'm going to."

172

"All right—all right." Emery felt ashamed.

"When the news got around that your dad had the flu, Em," Bunce said, "the big producers decided that now was the best time to act. Muller told Mary's dad to insist to Jim Lane that the directors' meeting be held at once, and Biggart gave Bullock the same orders."

"Okay," said Emery impatiently. "What comes next?"

They were descending the slope to the yard now.

"If Bullock, Mary's father and I—and probably Hollis and any other little dairyman the big producers can put the squeeze on—dump our stock," Bunce went on to explain, "that'll mean that the remaining Co-op membership will have to raise a lot of money in the next sixty days to absorb it."

The meaning of this stock-dumping at this particular time hit Emery hard. He knew that his father had borrowed against future milk checks to take care of March first debt payments. Probably most of the dairymen in the Co-op were similarly tied up. The membership would be in no position to raise money to buy up the turned-in stock.

"Now you can understand why Bullock bought up Co-op stock," Del said. "Biggart put up the money. And I didn't know at the time why I was urged to buy ten shares. Muller let me have the money. The big fellows have been planning this move for several months."

Bunce stopped talking to get his breath; then he resumed: "If Bullock, Mary's dad and I, and probably a few others, pull our milk out of the Co-op, the station won't be able to fill a tanker a day and that'll mean hauling at a loss."

They had reached the yard and Emery halted. In spite of the cold he was sweating. The mounting threats to the Co-op seemed to be smothering him and he unzipped his coat and flung the parka off his head.

Del Bunce faced him. "After Muller talked to me," he said, "I called my dad at home. He told me that the A.D. will buy the Co-op station at a price that will give the members six per cent interest on their investment. Bullock has that offer in his pocket for tonight's directors' meeting, and he's going to propose that the Co-op sell."

Bunce kicked at a lump of snow before continuing: "With your dad sick, he can get the two-thirds vote of the directors to pass it. Hollis and Carsen will side with him and Mr. Spivac. Of course the whole membership will have to pass on it, but the A.D. figures that after the Co-op tries to raise the money to buy up the dumped stock, and after the station runs at a loss for a month, they'll be willing to take the A.D.'s offer. Besides, the A.D. is promising to take back all the Co-op members except Nels Peterson, Jim Lane, and you and your dad. You four will be blacklisted."

Emery leaned heavily against the yard gate as if someone had hit him; then he straightened slowly. "What's *your* game, anyhow?" He dropped his head a little, glaring at Bunce.

"My game is trying to get my own dairy; it's the same game as yours," replied Del evenly.

Emery grabbed his coat front. "Then you're going to dump your stock?" His voice was hoarse and angry.

"Not if the rest of you will put up a fight to save the Co-op," said Bunce.

"Well . . ." Emery's hand dropped and he took a slow breath. "I'm sorry I ever called you a stooge for Muller."

"I earned it, I guess," said Del. "I can tell more."

"We'd better start doing something now," urged Mary.

They ran up the path to the house. In the dining room, Emery told David to get into his outdoor clothes and tend the syrup fire. Mrs. Crane came out of the downstairs bedroom looking startled.

"What's the matter, Emery?"

"We have to talk to Dad, Mom."

"Come in, Em," Mr. Crane called.

Emery told him what was happening. He listened quietly, looking pale, coughing heavily once or twice.

"What should we do next, Dad?" Emery asked.

Mr. Crane muttered: "If—I—were only on my feet." Then he wearily closed his eyes a moment, thinking. When he opened them again, he said: "The only way is to bring this to a head now. The A.D. hopes to squeeze the Co-op members and wear down their resistance to sell, all the time dangling in front of them this chance to make a six per cent profit . . ." He broke off, out of breath.

"We could call the whole membership together for a meeting tonight," Emery said.

"If only one or two of the others could be persuaded not to dump their stock," continued Mr. Crane, "like Del here." He glanced up at Mary. "Do you think your father might be talked out of selling his shares?"

"I don't know." She spoke in a low tone. "He's talked about letting the bank and Muller take everything."

Mr. Crane winced; then said to Emery: "See if you can call the membership together for a meeting."

Emery went to the telephone and began to call Co-op members: "This is Emery Crane. My dad has the flu. Bullock, Spivac, Hollis, and Carsen have forced Jim Lane to call the directors' meeting ahead of schedule. They're planning to put through a resolution to sell the Co-op to the A.D. Can you come down to the station to a meeting immediately?" Occasionally he answered a few questions; sometimes he added: "It's real urgent. Get down there as soon as you can."

Mary and Bunce checked the members he called against a membership list. It was after eight o'clock when he finished, and the three returned to the bedroom.

"They're coming, Dad," Emery informed him.

"Fine. Now go down there and do your best."

"I think we can lick them," Bunce promised, and the three went out to his car. He sent it roaring down the drive.

As they turned on to Route 20 toward Atlas, Emery asked: "What'll Muller do to you for this, Del?"

"Try to break me." Bunce's attention was fixed on his driving.

"And what about your dad? He's manager of the A.D.!" Emery hadn't thought about that angle and now it startled him.

"You didn't believe me when I said I wasn't stooging for Muller any more," Bunce said. "But last fall I really got fed up. And I have a card to play that Muller doesn't know about." The speeding car skidded a little and he brought it under control.

"Ever since you fellows started the Co-op," he continued, "my dad's been getting it from all sides as manager of the A.D. He never liked to do the things he has to do there—reject milk to soften up little dairymen so they'll take a price-cut, and a lot of other little dirty tricks just to help the big producers. But there wasn't much he could do about it. He had to have a job. Then Muller decided to start me out dairying just to help make the pinch on the Co-op bigger. That's given me a chance and my dad too."

They were going down the hill to the station. "My dad can quit the A.D. now," Del went on. "He can sell the home place in Sheltonville and he and Mother can move out to my dairy. With the money Dad has saved plus the money he gets for our house, I think we can pay Muller off—pay him off in time. That is, if the Co-op survives."

They pulled into the Co-op station yard. Only the directors' cars were there. When they entered the station they heard angry voices in the office, and Emery opened the door without knocking. The directors stared at the three in surprise. Jim Lane, looking harassed, suddenly took a deep breath. Nels Peterson grinned.

Bullock nodded his shaggy head at Del Bunce as if he'd been expecting him; then he turned to Lane: "I move that the chairman ask the visitors to leave the meeting."

Hollis seconded the motion. Lane called for a vote. Bullock, Hollis, and Carsen voted in favor; Spivac kept his eyes on the table but indicated his vote with a wave of his gnarled hand. Peterson continued to grin and didn't bother to vote.

Emery didn't wait for Jim Lane to tell him to leave. "Before we leave," he said, "I just want to say there'll be a meeting of the full membership here in a few minutes."

Jim Lane searched Emery's face and a faint smile grew around his lips. Bullock's cheeks turned a purplish red.

"Meeting—members," he stammered. Then his eyes hardened and he growled: "All right. We'll finish this off tonight. As good a time as later."

Nels Peterson ran his fingers through his graying hair excitedly. But Hollis seemed to shrink up in his chair; Spivac didn't move a muscle; and Homer Carsen's bushy moustache twitched violently.

Emery, Mary, and Bunce left the office. Cars were already arriving in the yard and they went to turn on the lights in the big room; then Emery stood at the door directing the members into the station.

The directors joined the meeting. Jim Lane called the crowd to order and asked Sam Rudnek to call the roll. Everyone was present except Lou Crane and Harold Shontz. Then Lane asked Emery to tell the reason for this meeting, but Bullock interrupted, demanding the right to speak.

"You might as well hear it straight," he said, and told them that Hollis, Spivac, Bunce, and he were withdrawing from the Co-op and turning in their shares—forty-three shares all together. "That's forty-three hundred dollars you'll have to raise in sixty days," he said.

The crowd listened in silence. He went on to explain

that without the milk from these four dairies, the Co-op would operate at a loss. Then he told them that the A.D. would take them all back and buy out the Co-op station, giving six per cent on their investment.

A murmur rose and died in the crowd.

"The board of directors has considered this offer carefully," Bullock said, "and has passed a resolution recommending the acceptance of the A.D. offer. Now I make a motion that this resolution be put before the whole membership."

His motion wasn't seconded at once and he glared at Hollis, who muttered weakly, "Second the motion."

"Discussion!" snapped Jim Lane fiercely.

"Mr. Chairman," called Emery, "we've had only Mr. Bullock's statement that the members he named intend to dump their stock and withdraw from the Co-op. I suggest that you ask each of the three named to speak for himself."

Several voices called, "Ask 'em, Jim."

"All right, let's hear from Del Bunce," said Lane.

Emery saw Del's face glistening with perspiration.

"I'm not going to dump my stock," he said distinctly. A few of the members cheered and he continued with a stronger voice: "Muller told me this evening to dump my Co-op stock, but I decided not to take orders from him any longer." Now a real cheer went up.

Emery noticed Mary working through the crowd to her father's side.

Bunce had not finished yet. "While I'm talking, I'll clear up some mysteries for you dairymen. I've a confession to make. I was the one who put the bad milk in your

cans in the unlocked coolers last summer. Muller and
Biggart talked me into that. I thought it was quite a joke
then. Now I see it as a dirty trick I'll be ashamed of for
a long time." He hung his head, his tongue moistening
dry lips.

"You'd better shut up!" Bullock yelled across the room.

"And I know all about the attempt to blow up the
Co-op station last spring before it opened," Bunce continued, ignoring Bullock. "I didn't make the try, but I
was there when one of the A.D. helpers did."

The crowd was shocked into silence by this information.

"You'll pay for this!" shouted Bullock. "And the A.D.'ll
fix your old man!"

An angry murmur started in the crowd, but Jim Lane
broke in on it: "Jack Spivac. How about you, Jack?"

Again Bullock yelled: "Muller'll sell you out if you
renege, Jack."

Emery, standing on tiptoes, saw Mary help her father
to get up from his seat on one of the milk pipelines.

"I won't dump mine," he said slowly. "Bullock's right
when he says Muller will sell me out. He'll eventually
dump my stock for me but that'll take time. That'll give
the Co-op time to raise the money to buy it." He sank
down heavily again.

"What about you, Mike Hollis?" called Lane.

Hollis didn't say anything; he just shook his head.

"I'm dumping mine—twenty-two shares," shouted Bullock, "and you'd better have the money ready in sixty
days." He pushed through the crowd toward the door.

A Co-op member near Emery muttered: "And we

thought Bullock bought up all that stock just to help the Co-op."

Homer Carsen didn't wait for Jim Lane to call on him. "There's no fool like an old fool," he said to the crowd. "And I'm sure an old one. Charlie Bullock told me that the A.D. was going to take us all back and stop playing tricks on us like they did last summer rejecting our milk for no reason, and we'd all make a nice profit out of the deal. I can see now that it was all a put-up job. I'm mighty glad these kids squashed the whole scheme. Now I move that the resolution to sell the Co-op be tabled."

His motion was seconded by a chorus. Jim Lane called for a vote and it was passed by a wild shout.

Emery asked to be allowed to say something. "I move that a committee be appointed by the chairman to help Mr. Spivac save his dairy if he'll accept the Co-op's help."

That motion was carried quickly, and Jim Lane called down: "Jack, will you let the Co-op help you out of your jam?"

Spivac rose unsteadily, leaning on Mary. "Thanks. I don't want to give up my place unless I have to."

Emery saw tears in Mr. Spivac's eyes and tears glistening on Mary's cheeks. He glanced away and noticed Del Bunce standing in the shadow of a big storage tank. Without hesitation he signaled for recognition from Jim Lane and proposed a vote of thanks to Del Bunce for his service to the Co-op.

The crowd didn't wait for the motion to pass; they surged around Del, shaking his hand, slapping him on the back. His tricks of last summer were already forgotten. Jim Lane had a hard time bringing the meeting to order again so that they could pass on to some important business.

Bullock as a director had to be replaced and George Kressel was voted into his spot on the board; then the meeting adjourned.

Del Bunce took Emery home.

"We've still got a fight ahead of us before grass time," Emery said, as Bunce let him out in the yard.

"Don't I know it," replied Del grimly. "But we've got the edge now."

"We'll lick the A.D. for good this time," Emery said. He extended his hand into the car and Bunce shook it firmly. "Thanks for the lift, Co-operator."

"Don't mention it," replied Del.

He drove off and Emery went up to the house to report to his father.

Chapter Twenty-four

GRASS TIME

The big roller end doors of the barn on the old Armstrong place were open to the dawn. Emery set the machine for the last of his cows to be milked, fitted the hose to the nozzle of the suction line, and turned the valve. After setting the teat-cups, he listened a moment to the pink-tuck, pink-tuck rhythm of the pulsator.

He had no electricity here—someday he'd have electricity, he assured himself—and his milker was powered by a sputtering gasoline engine. The sound drowned out the whistling of bluebirds along the lane and the song of a robin in the big maple back of the milkhouse. A thick

183

mist filled the valley, hiding the budding trees, and the sun was just a golden disk on the ridge above Atlas.

Satisfied that the milker was working as it should, Emery took a milk pail and stool and stepped in beside the cow the machine had just finished.

"So, bossy," he said. "So, Ivy." He began stripping, and the cow turned her head in the stanchion and mooed at him. "Yeah, yeah," he said to her, "nice bossy. Mary hasn't been to see you lately, has she?" He began whistling to himself.

When the milking was finished and the gasoline engine shut off, the dairy became suddenly and strangely silent. As if to correct that strangeness, his whistling grew louder, and when he freed the cows from their stanchions, he shouted: "Ho, there, get going!"

It was grass time again and the herd ambled along the lane toward the lower meadow.

After closing the gate, Emery returned to the barn and paused a moment in the doorway, looking back into the mist-covered fields: his fields, his cows. He took a deep breath and started through the barn: his barn too. Well, none of them were quite his. He had only an equity in them, but they would be all his in three or four years.

He dumped the last milker tank through the strainer into one of four cans at the upper end of the alleyway, then looked to see how nearly full it was. Two-thirds full. He'd made almost four cans this morning and four last night—almost eight cans to go to the Co-op station.

Yes, he assured himself, this place would be his in a few years, all his, because the Co-op was solid.

The A.D. had quit fighting after that Co-op meeting

in late February. On the first of March, Del Bunce's dad resigned as manager of the A.D. But before he left, he told the small dairymen still bringing milk to the A.D. station why he was pulling out as manager and gave them plenty of reasons why they should pull out as patrons. And by the middle of March, enough small dairymen had come over to the Co-op to take up all the stock Charlie Bullock had dumped.

Emery washed up the milker and put it on the rack to dry, then loaded his four cans on the truck standing by the milkhouse window and started for home. When he passed the small four-room house near the road, he thought: one of these days I ought to fix it up to go with the rest of the buildings. But once he had passed it, he concluded that there was no hurry. He found it more convenient to live at home.

Mr. Crane and David were just finishing the milking at the home barn when he pulled the truck up to the milkhouse and began loading on the milk from the cooler.

"Almost eight cans for me this morning," he shouted.

"Guess you'll make it by the time the milk's in full flood," replied his father.

David came up from turning the cows out to grass and said: "Hey, Em, how about giving your herd a bacteria test. You ought to have them checked one of these days."

"Okay," replied his brother. "Come over when you want to and make your check."

They went up to the house to breakfast. It was a big meal—pancakes, eggs, bacon, cereal and coffee—a big meal to start off a big day's work. And when the family finished,

Emery leaned back and remarked appreciatively: "Gee, Mom, I'm glad I have a place close enough to home so I can eat here. I'd never get filled up otherwise."

His mother smiled. "Oh, I guess Mary could fill you up."

David let out a whoop of laughter, Mr. Crane grinned slyly, and Emery's face grew a deep apple-red.

He glared at his brother. "You'd better shut up, bug hunter, or I won't give you a chance to check my cows."

They left the house and Emery went whistling down to the truck to haul the milk to the Co-op station. Mary was waiting in her father's pickup to get the empties. Emery waved to her, unloaded his cans quickly, and drove over to the other end of the line to wait with her.

"Made almost eight cans," he boasted.

"That's fine," she answered, her face glowing.

They saw Del Bunce coming toward them, grinning broadly. "Good news. Three more have pulled out of the A.D. Leo Reilly's come back to the Co-op."

"Gee, we're really growing now," said Emery.

"Sam says the Co-op's putting on another tanker to haul the milk during the flood," continued Bunce; then he grinned at Emery and asked: "Well, how's the *little* dairy farmer this morning?"

"Feeling great." He grinned back. "And how's the *big* dairy farmer?"

"Muller's still breathing down our necks," replied Bunce soberly. "But he can't corner us now that the Co-op's solid."

The Spivac empties came down the conveyor and they loaded them on Mary's truck. Before she drove away, she said to Emery: "Dad's supposed to get some papers today that your father will have to go over. I'll bring them over." Then she drove out of the station yard and up the street.

Emery knew that the papers she spoke of had to do with the re-financing of her father's farm through the Co-op. This was the work of the committee appointed at the big meeting in February to save the Spivacs from Muller. His father was one of the committee men. At the last general Co-op meeting, a resolution had been passed which established the committee as a permanent part of the Co-op organization with the function of helping any Co-op dairyman in trouble. That was another factor which made the Co-op solid.

When Emery got home, he took his father's tractor and disk harrow and began to prepare one of the fields on the old Armstrong place for oats. That was another advantage he had in running this farm close to home; he could use his father's machinery in return for helping his father with the farm work. As he finished the piece, he remembered that Mary had said she was bringing some papers over this evening.

Just as he was finishing the milking she rode into the yard on Dolly and up to the barn; she dropped the reins and swung to the ground. Without hesitating, she walked down the alleyway behind the cows and up beside the cow Ivy, talking to her, scratching the base of her black ears.

Emery finished stripping the last cow and shut off the gasoline engine. When the dairy grew quiet, he said: "You ought to come oftener—she'd give more milk."

She smiled at him over the back of the cow, her eyes sparkling. "Ivy still remembers me—I'm sure she does."

"How could she forget you," he answered and she made a face at him. Then he gestured proudly toward the four cans in the alleyway. "Full, all four of 'em. And some besides."

She joined him and took the milking machine out of his hands. "You let the cows out; I'll wash up the milker."

"Oh, I can do it," he protested.

She paid no attention to him and started across the yard to the milkhouse. He watched her go; then, whistling, he freed the cows from their stanchions and swept the dairy floor. He was loading the full cans on to the truck to take them over to the cooler in his father's milkhouse when Mary finished her job and rejoined him, drying her hands.

"Thanks," he said. "That's a chore I don't care much about doing."

"I don't mind it," she replied smiling. "I always do it at home." She began feeling through her jacket pockets, and brought out a large envelope. "Here, before I forget it. Will you give this to your dad? It's those papers I spoke of." Then she caught up Dolly's reins and prepared to mount.

"I'll take care of it," he said, watching her swing into the saddle.

As he walked beside her up the drive, past the house on the old Armstrong farm, she asked: "Will you let me look inside sometime, Em?"

"Sure." Her interest puzzled him. "Want to now?"

"No. I haven't time now. Sometime though. It looks as if it could be made into a nice home."

"Oh sure, it can be fixed up."

"So long," she said. "See you at the Co-op in the morning." Then, touching Dolly lightly with her heels, she galloped out of the yard and up the road.

He watched her go, his forehead puckered a little. Then he returned to the truck to drive home. As he swung the machine out of the yard and his glance swept over the little house, he thought: on the first rainy day I ought to get in there and clean that place up. Then he remembered Mary's saying that it could be made into a nice home. Plans sprang into his mind: four nice rooms, a wing could be added to the west, a new porch could be put on—it *could* make a nice home. This thinking brought a smile to his lips but he didn't know he was smiling.

When he pulled the truck up to the loading window of his father's milkhouse, David was inside lowering cans of milk into the cooler. He stared up at his brother.

"What're you grinning about?" he demanded.

"Nothing," Emery replied, suddenly conscious of the smile on his face. He tried to stop smiling but his smile only grew broader. "Grass time, isn't it? I guess a fellow has a right to do a little dreaming."